TEN TANGLED TALES

BECAUSE LIFE'S NO FAIRY TALE

SUDUHITA MITRA SANKHE

Illustrated by
SOURABH SANKHE

PRAISE FOR - TEN TANGLED TALES

"INTRIGUING COLLECTION WITH A SURPRISING TWIST. HIGHLY RECOMMENDED FOR LITERATURE COLLECTIONS FOR THE CONTEMPORARY INDIAN WRITINGS."

- Midwest Book Reviews

"SUDUHITA HAS BEAUTIFULLY PENNED THE VARIOUS FACETS OF HUMAN LIFE IN URBAN SOCIETIES THROUGH LOVE, MARRIAGE, AGONY, JEALOUSY, CONSPIRACY AND HUMAN PSYCHOLOGY."

-Prof. Tamo Mibang, Former Vice Chancellor, Rajiv Gandhi Central University

"IT IS A SHORT STORY READER'S DELIGHT! ALL STORIES COVER A RANGE OF EMOTIONS, EXPERIENCES AND SETTINGS; GIVING ONE THE SENSATION OF SEEING A GREAT DEAL OF THE WORLD AND THE PEOPLE WHO INHABIT IT, WITHOUT MOVING AN INCH. A GREAT SATISFYING COLLECTION ALL IN ALL!"

- Ushasi Sen Basu – Author Kathputli & A Killer Amongst Us

"THE STORIES ARE MYSTERIOUS AND SOMETIMES SPINE TINGLING. IT WAS A JOY TO READ."

- Darya Crockett - Ebook Launch

TEN TANGLED TALES

Author:
SUDUHITA MITRA SANKHE

Ten Tangled Tales is a work of fiction. Names, characters, places, and incidents are the product of author's imagination or are used fictitiously. Any resemblance to actual persons, living or dead, events, or locales is entirely coincidental.

www.suduhitamitra.com

Edited By: Ebook Launch Editors
Book designed in Canva and illustrations edited in Imaengine.

To everyone who has a story within : May you find your happily ever after!

&

to my happily ever afters - Mom,Dad, Sourabh,K&R

TEN TANGLED TALES

Once upon a time...

Beneath a dreary sky...

CONTENTS

"*I* really like this guy. He is tall, handsome, and a doctor."

"Then you marry him, MOM…I am really not interested!" Riya said through gritted teeth.

Two pairs of wide glossy eyes zoomed in on Riya instantly. Riya knew she had crossed that invisible line with her statement, but somedays such talks infuriated her no end. She could feel the impending question—*"When will you get married?"*—looming in the backdrop. Nothing at this point would make her mom change the topic. She looked away from the photograph that her mom had laid on the table.

"Why are you so against marriage? I really don't get you sometimes!" muttered her mom sullenly as she served lunch.

Riya sighed.

This was not the first time she was having this conversation with her mom. Every weekend they would have the same disagreements, and these talks were getting on Riya's nerves lately. When Riya moved out of her parents' home to live near her workplace, she thought it would be liberating. But somehow, she was stuck with these weekly luncheons with her mom now. It had started as a normal weekly meeting over some good home-cooked meals, but as weeks went by, things changed. Riya soon realized that this was an emotional ploy to keep the conversations alive about the eligible bachelors in town

She was a perfectly normal and a well-educated girl. She had friends, a loving family, and a stable job. Just because she had reached that thirty-something age, everyone she met only enquired about that one thing missing in her life—a husband. She had tried giving the age-old tradition of arranged marriage a chance, but the more she met those men and their families, the more distraught she became with their unending questions and demands. She now wanted to settle down on her own terms with a guy who she clicked with.

Recently, her roommate introduced her to the world of online dating, and she was drawn to that idea. It at least sounded so much better than the typical "arranged marriage" scenario that her mother had presented her with. The only hiccup was breaking this news to her mom without breaking her heart.

"Look, Mom...I have nothing against marriage! I would love to get married to someone I like. I just hate this *arranged* process. I don't want to parade in front of the prospective groom's families like I am some commodity up for sale. It feels so degrading," Riya said earnestly, her face showed signs of mild exhaustion.

"What's degrading in meeting a family? It worked for me when I was your age. I don't think there is a better process."

This was exactly what Riya wanted her mom to say. The bait had worked better than she had anticipated. Now all she had to do was hook her into it completely.

"Umm…I think there is a better process, Mom," Riya said softly. A smile crossed her lips momentarily, but she tried to hide it before her mom suspected foul play. "Don't get mad, but my roommate already hooked me on to some of those online dating sites. I really want to try this and see. I have a feeling it might just work!" Riya pleaded.

Her mom scrunched her eyebrows for a moment but didn't say a word.

Does it mean she is okay with it? Riya wondered.

They both ate their lunch in silence, and Riya didn't utter a word either. She couldn't comprehend what her mom was thinking.

Silence is better than an argument any day, she thought.

After a long pause, her mom shook her head and added, "I really don't understand your generation. If you think it might work, try it out. You are not going to listen to me anyway!!" Her mom shrugged. "And… don't come crying back to me when this online stuff fails!"

Riya continued to listen to her mom's warnings without a word because contradicting her at this point might just take away the faint approval that Riya had just received. This was how her mom always approved things. It was never a straightforward yes from her. It was always supplemented with some words of caution.

The truth is that Riya herself was not sure if this online dating would work out. She was not even sure what exactly she was looking for in a guy. All she knew was she didn't want to end up with those boring tweed-suited guys that her mom usually picked. She wanted a companion and not just some means for a social escape.

Was Mom ever really happy with her arranged marriage? she wondered most times, but never dared to ask.

Her mom was married to a high-profile business-man. But Riya rarely had her dad around while growing up. He was always traveling for his job being the sole earner. Although she was used to meeting him on occasional get-togethers, she did not want to end up with a husband like that. She had seen the struggles that her mom had to go through, and Riya was sure that she couldn't do half of what her mom did, to raise her all by herself.

She decided to bide her time, fervently hoping that some magical meet-cute was on the cards for her soon. All she had to do was keep checking the profiles and swipe left or right from her phone. These dating applications had made life so much easier—swipe right if you like and swipe left if you don't. Everything else would be taken care of by the algorithm, and for a change, Riya wanted to place her trust on something that had some logic behind their matchmaking skill.

Luckily for her, Ajay Joshi happened soon enough. Riya had been swiping left on most profiles of men. It was not like she didn't like how they looked or what their profile description said, but somewhere, she felt that these chiseled guys were just too perfect for her. Ajay was probably the only guy she had swiped right to. His profile was pretty ordinary, but what caught her eye was a messy pile of books that lay in the background of his otherwise boring profile picture. Something about that mundane picture told Riya that he was a genuine person, as he was not trying to hide his real self like all the other guys, who had photoshopped themselves to look like some movie stars.

As she swiped right, she typed an introductory cheesy text to Ajay: "You do seem like a messy bookworm. Any interest in meeting another one?" and hit send.

A few hours later, he replied.

"Another bookworm is using this app!! PEST ALERT! Anyway, what book are you latched onto these days?" Ajay texted.

Riya smiled.

This might have been the most cliched way to start a conversation, but she was happy that someone asked her about a book instead of *"So...what do you do?"* Riya had a tough time opening about herself to complete strangers. About books, she knew she could talk more openly.

"I am almost through *Only Love Is Real* now. What are you onto, Mister?" she at once texted back.

"What a coincidence!! I am reading the same book: *Only Love Is Real—The Story of Soulmates United!*"

"Are you kidding me!! Both of us are reading the book on past lives. That is some coincidence!" Riya could feel the excitement building in her already.

For a minute, she totally forgot that she was texting a total stranger. She had rarely encountered a moment when someone she knew was reading the exact same book as she was.

Destiny must be at play or is it some past life bond? she thought as her heart fluttered.

They ended up exchanging hundreds of texts throughout the day on that note. Their chats, which had started with a small coincidence, ended with a list of pleasant surprises.

Riya soon realized that they had so much in common when it came to books, but when it came down to the topic of the 'books turned into movies', their views were poles apart.

It completely made sense when one of them suggested that they exchange numbers and start arguing on the phone instead. It would be so much easier to vocally debate on their disagreements than typing in lengthy chats.

All through the night, they spent a good amount of time disputing each other's argument. But amidst all this, somewhere deep inside, Riya felt a sudden sense of happiness that her first right swipe had crossed her paths with someone who she could at least relate to. Never had Riya felt so comfortable in the company of a total stranger.

After that night, they spoke to each other every day.

"I just don't get it. How can you not believe in ghosts!!" Ajay exclaimed one day during their usual conversation.

"And you really believe that ghosts are just trying to scare us with creaking doors and howling winds?" Riya laughed at Ajay's girlish trait.

"C'mon, ghosts are real, Riya!! What do you think happens to our souls when we die?" Ajay interjected.

"They become energies…not ghosts!!"

"So…you believe in energies?"

"Umm yeah…what's your point?" Riya questioned.

"Exactly my point. Negative energy is nothing, but ghosts and positive energy become angels!"

"Noooo...this is stupid!!" Riya tried to contradict, but she couldn't find a better argument.

"*TO-MAY-TO, TO-MAH-TO*!! Same thing but pronounced differently. In short, you too believe in ghosts!! I rest my case now." Ajay sniggered away, leaving Riya smiling.

There was no denying that they had more similarities than either of them had ever anticipated finding on their dates. Even the differences they had, seemed to complement each other in a myriad of ways. Ajay, who liked to be called AJ, was a smooth talker and a carefree adventurer, leading an old-school life, while Riya was a little uptight, prissy, and tech-savvy, but both of them had a benevolent heart and a great sense of humor.

They were grateful to the dating algorithm that made their paths cross. But the more she talked with him, the more it became evident to her that destiny was at play too. They had grown up in two different cities, with a completely different background, and hardly had any chance of encountering each other. AJ was a bank manager and had just moved from Lucknow to Pune, India, a few months back, whereas Riya was a research associate in the Microbiology Department at Pune University. They were so different, and yet they could feel that invisible bond between them growing strong with every second.

They had just been talking on the phone for a few weeks now, but somehow it felt like he had been that missing piece in her otherwise perfect life. So, when AJ asked Riya out for coffee, it felt just normal.

Riya picked a casual outfit but paired it with a rich scarf to complement her wheatish complexion. This was her first real date in years, and she wanted to look exquisite even though they were meeting in a small eatery called Durga Coffee. It was both their favorite cold coffee location in Pune. Although AJ was pretty new to Pune, having stayed all his life in Lucknow, he seemed to know the really good eating joints here, and Riya was glad that they had this in common too.

Pune was an eclectic mix of a growing city and an old township. It was a place filled with upscale sky towers and also had small streetside joints to sit, eat, and relax. As Riya got out of the taxi, she could feel the silent ways the city always seemed to mirror her feelings. Looking around, she could feel the cool breeze and the softening mix of smiles all around her. Her eyes caught the familiar face of AJ waiting for her amidst the crowd. Although this was their first in-person meeting, she immediately recognized his dark textured face and that heartwarming smile from his picture. In person, she found AJ even more friendly and loquacious. To her surprise, he had already ordered coffee for them.

"How did you know this is my favorite beverage here?" she exclaimed, looking at the tall glass of cold coffee waiting for her on the table.

"I guessed this would be the drink of choice for all bookworms!!" Ajay winked at her as he raised his glass of cold coffee.

For the next few hours, Riya lost track of time. She didn't notice that the sun had long set, the scenery had changed, and the crowd around them had thinned. She was too engrossed in their conversations that she didn't care where she was anymore. Usually, Riya had to come up with a narrative of herself, that she shared with men, during their first meeting. But with AJ there was this weird connection that made her comfortable in her own skin. Even though she was four years older than him, neither of them felt that it mattered anymore. AJ had also opened up completely, sharing things that made him vulnerable. No one around them could have guessed that it was their first date. There was an accelerated intimacy for both of them, and it took them by surprise. As their date came to an end, they just held onto each other's hands for a long time, wondering how this miracle happened.

"Do you think it's too soon to feel this way?" Riya asked as they walked back home hand in hand.

"I wish I had met you sooner," AJ replied as he pulled her closer.

They walked in silence, glowing in the subtle warmth of their young love.

After that night, it was like their relationship fast-forwarded to a year-old maturity. It had been only a month, but they were completely inseparable—always hooked onto the phone or with each other. They had done almost everything in a month that couples usually take years to do. They had even met each other's friend circle and had traveled to multiple places on weekend hiking trips. Neither of them expected a formal proposal because their compatibility spoke for itself. It was just a matter of time before marriage would happen. The only thing remaining was meeting the parents.

"I think I am going to tell my mom about us. What do you think?" Riya asked one morning as she lay in bed watching AJ making coffee.

"I have a better plan. Why don't we both meet her for lunch tomorrow?" AJ said.

Riya immediately picked up her phone and started to text her mom.

"You always have the best suggestions, babe. I love you for that!" she said as she blew him a kiss.

AJ smiled and handed Riya a cup of coffee. Riya's phone buzzed again.

"So, tomorrow lunch it is," she said as she flipped her phone to him to show him the text from her mom. "By the way, when can I meet your parents? They must be in Lucknow, right?" she looked at AJ questioningly.

AJ had never brought up his parents in all their conversations so far, and Riya was not sure why. The sooner they met each other's parents, the sooner they could get married.

"Umm...my parents are dead," AJ said after a momentary pause.

"Oh, I am so sorry, AJ!!!" Riya put her cup down as she held his hand. "You never said anything...I should have guessed," she mumbled. "By the way, can I ask what happened?" Riya tried to sound apologetic and remorseful in subtle ways, but her inquisitiveness still got the better of her.

He sighed and nodded.

"Well… I don't really know if they are dead. Truth is, I don't know who my parents are."

Riya stared in disbelief.

He put his cup down and held her hands as he looked into her eyes.

"Look, Riya…I don't like to talk about this because I was raised at an orphanage in Lucknow." Ajay hesitated a little, shook his head, and then looked away.

"Uh…you know I don't care about your upbringing, right?" Riya asked, despite the shocking and sudden revelation. She wanted to let Ajay know that he could tell her everything without the fear of being judged.

AJ nodded.

"That's why I stopped asking about my parents long back," he added after a brief pause. "I don't know who they are, and I have no intention of finding them either. They left me at the hospital when I was born, and the hospital folks handed me off to the orphanage. It has been thirty years, and no one ever came looking for me. For all I know, they are dead. So, the orphanage has always been my home. But... If you want, I can take you there to meet the warden, Mrs. Joshi. She took good care of us, and gave us a name and her surname"

His feeble attempt to joke made Riya smile. She held his hands, not knowing what else to say. She would have never guessed that such a happy-go-lucky guy had such a tragic story buried underneath him. Deep in her heart, she didn't want AJ to live a life of being an orphan when his parents might still be out there looking for him.

"I don't think you should give up," Riya muttered. "You know there are ways to track your parents through DNA, right?" She said after a brief pause.

"Ah... The molecular biologist has spoken at last!" he smiled.

"I am not joking, AJ. It is a real thing. I can hook you up with some really good companies who do it. We can get some university discounts too," she said.

"Thanks, but the truth is I don't want to find them," he said curtly and walked away from her.

Riya was aghast. She couldn't fathom how AJ could be so nonchalant about his parents. Although she admired him more for making it all on his own and leading a successful and independent life, saying that your parents were dead was a little theatrical for her. Also, these days, with technology it was not that difficult to trace people.

Why doesn't he want to find them? she thought silently but decided to convince him to change his mind.

She followed him to the living room and showed him her Gen-e profile (pronounced as genie) on her phone, where she had taken a swab test to understand her genetic disposition better.

"Look at this. All you need to do is take a swab and download this app. They tell you everything else." Riya shoved her phone into his reluctant hands.

The mobile application was her account that was customized to show only her genetic results. It was pretty colorful, showing all the red areas that she needed to watch out for because her genes were weak when it came to diseases like diabetes or conditions such as migraines. There was also a section called Relative Finder, which had a family tree based on the shared segments of her DNA with others. She had her mom and dad listed there along with some of her cousins. She had the highest shared DNA with her mom and dad at 50%. The percentage of shared DNA decreased when it came to cousins.

AJ glanced at it, but he didn't look impressed.

"I know what it does, Riya... You don't have to explain everything to me like I am some child. I just don't want to do all this," AJ said vehemently.

Riya bit her lips. She didn't want to sound rude, but sometimes AJ could be a thick-headed rigid person. In this modern day of technology, he sometimes behaved in a very old-fashioned manner, and she was aware of this trait of his. She was certain that only her persistence could get through to him.

"What if your parents are out there still looking for you? Wouldn't you want to meet them then?" Riya reasoned.

"It doesn't take thirty years to find someone!" AJ removed the hand that she had placed on his arm, and he walked out again.

This was the first time they were seriously arguing. Riya could feel the heat rise in her cheeks as she curled her fingers into a fist. She didn't know how to end this fight, or perhaps she didn't want to end it. Riya was sure that she had every right to know about his genetic constituents. They were going to have a life together, and genes defined everything.

Being a biologist herself, she appreciated such knowledge that gave her power over her own self. Whenever they found in their database that your DNA matched with someone in their database, they let you know about it and you could get in touch with that person and determine exactly where they fit in your family tree. Although it was a new concept in India, she didn't doubt it's efficacy. A lot of people were already trying this, which only meant that there was a chance that someone related to AJ might already be in the Gene-e database. And not just that, they could additionally use it to check their genetic compatibility. Riya believed that it was so much better than matching stars or horoscopes.

Riya followed AJ into the next room, hatching up the right words.

"Don't you care about our future? You don't even know your genetic elements! What will happen to our kids?" Riya tried to take a different trajectory.

"What? Kids!! You are thinking way ahead, Riya!!" AJ shook his head.

He briefly opened his lips to say something but not a word escaped. He shook his head as if holding back his true feelings. Instead, he ran his fingers through his hair and clasped the hair ends tightly.

Riya could see that his face was flushed with anger. She was irritated too, but she decided to take the high road instead of saying something that she might regret later.

If I want to convince him, I can't lose my cool, Riya told herself.

"Look AJ, you can just opt to study your genetic makeup. If you don't want to find your parents, I will completely respect that," Riya croaked softly.

AJ stood at one corner, facing away from her. He was still not sold on the whole of this idea. This was probably the first time both didn't see eye to eye. Riya could tell that they both were trying to control and assess their words before they came out of their lips. She waited patiently for him to respond.

After a long pause, he shrugged and faced Riya. He sighed and rolled his eyes. His face had suddenly lost that affable look that he usually had.

He sat down on the sofa as if giving up.

"Fine...I will do it." AJ breathed heavily. "But I have one condition. You see my results when they send it to me, and you do all the analysis with my genetic problems because I don't want to find my parents. Do we have a deal?" It was his turn to look at her questioningly.

Riya smiled and kissed him lightly on the forehead. It was their first disagreement, and it had ended in him caving. It was a victory that she had no intention of letting him know about.

The very next day she got him a Gen-e swab test box. It was a company that was not yet established in India. They just had their swab kits available in the Indian market. Riya would have to mail the swabs to the US, and the results would show up in a couple of weeks, either on email or on their mobiles, if the application was installed on the phones.

AJ did the swab test as he promised, but he declined to set up anything on his phone. In the form, he also declined the Relative Finder option, so that he wouldn't be informed if his DNA matched with someone else. But there was a caveat to this that Riya didn't bother sharing with AJ during their mini fight: if his DNA found a match with someone who had the relative finder turned on, they would still be notified about AJ's existence, and they could connect with him. That way, Riya could keep the hope alive of reuniting him with his parents one day. She packaged everything properly and dropped it off at the courier as they both made their way to meet her mom for lunch.

For the first time in her life, Riya enjoyed the luncheon with her mother. AJ was blending in well too. She had told him about her absentee father before their meeting, and AJ was nice enough not to bring him up at all in the conversation with her mom. Luckily for Riya, AJ's orphan lineage also didn't alarm her mom. She was in a happy state of mind, that her daughter had finally found the one she could settle down with.

"I will ask Riya's dad to talk to a priest and set a wedding date," Riya's mom added as they parted ways.

Riya wondered silently and smiled, *What did I do to deserve such a nice man! He makes love look too easy.*

As soon as the wedding preparations started, Riya and AJ got busy arranging and planning their wedding. The wedding date was set for in a month, which made it all the crazier. Every day, Riya thanked her lucky star because AJ was the biggest support system through all the wedding madness.

On her wedding day, Riya woke up to a buzzing phone. She rubbed her sleepy eyes as she scrolled through all her notifications. There were a couple of missed calls from her mom, which was normal. She always called her in the morning. Then there was a missed call from her dad too, and that kind of explained the two calls from her mom. He must be home for the wedding, and Mom must be feeling the pressure. But something else also caught her eye. There was a notification in her Gen-e account as well. She clicked on it as she yawned, wondering what it could be. She had never received any notification in there.

Her eyes widened when she read:

Found potential relative. Click here to update family tree.

She sat upright on her bed as the page loaded.

Riya Singh and Ajay Joshi have 27% DNA in common
Potential Relationship: *Half sibling/stepsibling*
Common Relation: *Rohan Singh*

Riya stared at the phone, wide-eyed, shaking her head.

"This can't be true! How can we both share DNA with *my* dad?" she mumbled as she checked Ajay Joshi's profile in the Gene-e app. All his details matched with the AJ she knew.

I am dating my stepbrother...Ewww!! she thought. *How could that have happened! Don't dating algorithms check for such things??*

Waves of nausea added to Riya's misery as she continued to process it. Her stomach lurched as she tried to control her desire to puke all over the report.

How could Dad not tell us that he had another child with someone else, or did he not know? All kinds of thoughts popped into Riya's mind, questioning the sanctity of her own family. None of this made any sense to her, and she struggled to wrap her head around it.

Just then her phone vibrated.

AJ calling!

It hid that report for a while, but it made her feel even more disgusted at herself. She couldn't even bring herself to answer it.

Thank God we are not married! she thought wryly.

She felt crippled with shame as tears started to roll down her cheeks. Her phone slid down her fingers, and she slipped back into her bed crying hysterically. Her perfect life with AJ had collapsed right in front of her eyes, revealing a dark family secret instead. She grabbed a pillow and screamed into it, muffling her sound but releasing her pain. After a long time, she pulled her face away from the pillow, wiped her tears, and decided to confront her parents about it.

And for AJ, she decided that this text message should suffice, as there was no way she could look him in the eye after this.

"Can't marry you. Our dad will explain."

HELLO SUNSHINE!

*D*eath was stalking the whole world. Everyone called it the COVID-19 (Corona Virus Disease-2019).

But Sana was preoccupied with other important matters. This could wait.

She and Jai had just moved to a new house in a new city with their five-year-old daughter Mili. Weeks later, the city went on a lockdown, and all nonessential workplaces were closed until further notice. They were still trying to settle down, but now they had to do so with extra caution. The virus was said to be a nasty one, and it had lingered on for months. All cities across the world were trying to cope with the mounting number of deaths, and locking the city down was an only alternative at that point. Everything happening around them was making their move difficult.

As I said, Sana had a lot of things on her mind, but COVID-19 wasn't one of them.

I met Sana just a day after the state of Minnesota went into lockdown. My house was right across the street from theirs. I was walking my dog, and she was playing with her daughter in the front yard.

"Welcome to Ridgewood," I said as I waved at her.

This neighborhood was a friendly one. We waved at one another and had small conversations. If we got along well, we even invited them over.

Luckily, Sana and I got along well on our first encounter and ended up talking for hours standing right on the streets maintaining the social distancing protocol of six feet. The CDC[1] had recommended that if we distanced ourselves from other people, we would be safe. So, the new normal was established at a six-feet distance.

She and Jai had moved all the way from Texas and were just starting to settle here.

Sana's brown eyes and brown hair gleamed in the morning sun as she chatted away about losing her restaurant job and how crazy things had been. Her daughter lay on the green grass drawing things in the air with her little hand. They both had the same kind of hair.

Like mother like daughter, I thought.

"This is all ridiculous. I think people are unnecessarily getting paranoid about this virus. What can a virus do?" she said.

I didn't agree with her. It had started as five cases three weeks back, but now there were thousands of them in the state. I thought it was scary. But then again you don't contradict your neighbors the first time you meet them. The first thing of being a friendly neighbor is you nod along and smile.

My dog, Simba, on the other hand was not aware of such manners. He growled as if not happy with the statement.

Mili heard the dog and came running to stand beside Sana. Her innocent eyes sparkled as she made cute noises trying to impress Simba.

"You have a lovely daughter," I said, trying to change the subject.

"Oh, thank you. Mili...say hi!" Sana said.

Mili shyly mumbled something, and then hid behind Sana again. She clutched onto Sana's scarf as if that were her invisible armor. I was finding Mili quite entertaining and only half listened to what Sana had to say.

"Her daycare closed last week, but luckily Jai was home to take care of her. It is so difficult to keep a five-year-old busy! Now that I am home, I am seeing stars," she rambled on.

"Does she draw?" I asked, remembering Mili trying to trace something in the blankness of the air.

"Oh yes, all the time." Sana gave a puzzled look.

"Get her some chalks and ask her to draw on the sidewalks." I suddenly remembered that all around the country, this was becoming a trend with cities after cities going into lockdown and people socially distancing themselves from everyone. Street art was becoming a means to spread the joy and a productive way to keep the kids busy. Sana seemed to like my idea. We parted on that because Simba was starting to get restless standing in one place during his walking routine.

I didn't bump into Sana for quite some time after that. But I saw Mili making rainbows, a sun, and clouds on the sidewalk lying on her stomach, her thin legs stretched out, her skinny left hand balancing her beautiful face and her right hand scribbling on the sidewalk. She was a cute kid, and this neighborhood didn't have a lot of them, so it made me happy every time I saw her.

"Hello, sunshine!" I would shout at her as I walked past her every morning.

She would look at me with some vague recognition, and then continue scribbling with her chalk.

Sometimes, I saw her talk alone as she drew faces, and I felt sorry for the little girl. The chaos in the whole world was creating more mental health issues than what we were ready to deal with. Human beings are, after all, social animals and they can't be caged. Asking them to stay at home and stay away from people was making everyone lonely and miserable. Children could adapt easily; for instance, Mili had resorted to an invisible friend when she craved company. Adults, on the other hand, resorted to bad influences, like the wine bottle on the hidden shelf, just to get through the day.

One day, as I was walking with Simba, I noticed that Mili was not at her usual place. She was probably up early because I could see some drawings on her spot already. I didn't realize that I had grown so fond of her that her absence kind of stirred me from within. I took a detour as I crossed the empty street, just to see her sketch.

I stood in awe as I looked at the faces that were drawn on the sidewalk. It was the face of Mr. and Mrs. Anderson—the old couple who lived a couple of houses down the street.

She is good, I silently praised her artistic hand.

Mili had captured Mrs. Anderson's curly hair and thick glasses etched on a plump face so well, and Mr. Anderson looked exactly like he did in real life—thin, wrinkled, and bald.

I decided to walk down to their house and tell Mr. and Mrs. Anderson to take a walk sometimes. I knew this sketch would cheer them up for sure. I felt joy within me like my own daughter had done this, but then again two weeks of no social lifestyle can make you more social in subtle ways sometimes.

I knocked at the Anderson family door, but there was no answer. I knocked again, and after a while, I heard some footsteps approaching. But the door did not open. I saw Mr. Anderson peeping out through their living room window. I found that a little weird, but I smiled and waved at him.

He waved back and disappeared behind the heavy curtain, leaving me all perplexed.

I must have caught them at the wrong time, I told myself.

I was about to leave when I saw him back with a notepad. On it, he had scribbled:

We have COVID-19. In quarantine. Can't come out.

I was stunned when I read this. I didn't have a notebook on me, so I shouted back "Take care and call me if you need anything!"

I gestured a phone with my hand, unsure if I was audible from outside.

He nodded, and I went back my way not knowing what to do with this information.

I decided to be more careful because the virus had finally entered our street. It was a weird feeling. It had been few months now, and we hardly knew anything concrete about the virus. Some said it spread through air, while others said it spread through contact. I didn't even know what precautionary measures I could take to protect myself. The only constant thing happening around the world was people were dying with flu-like symptoms, and there was no cure yet that could reduce the surmounting death rate. It had even been declared as a global pandemic, but a few continued to say that we were at a war with an invisible alien. There were too many conspiracy theories and old-school narratives out there, and I did not know what to believe anymore.

I went back and called all the people I knew in our neighborhood, told them about Mr. and Mrs. Anderson, and asked them to be more cautious. I didn't have Sana's number, so I decided to tell her if I bumped into her again.

I had reduced Simba's walks around the neighborhood and instead spent more time in our yard after that. I still saw Mili, sometimes wondering what she had drawn, but I dared not venture across the street with the virus around.

One night, I got a call from one of my neighbors, Mrs. Smith, who mentioned that Mr. and Mrs. Anderson succumbed to COVID-19 at the hospital that day. It was shattering to hear someone you know for so long fall victim to this deadly virus. The virus appeared more real than ever. Mrs. Smith was shaken too. She even told me that a few more cases had been detected in our beautiful locality.

"By the way, those new people who moved in across your place…their daughter is a freak I tell you!" Mrs. Smith added bluntly.

"Why would you say that?" I asked, shocked to hear such an allegation. Mili was nothing but a kid, doing her part in spreading cheer in this dark world. No one should call her a freak.

"Didn't you hear? Every face she draws ends up with COVID-19, and two of them even died. That's some freaky artwork!" she said in hushed tone.

"I don't think that's how it happened. She must have drawn the faces of people she had seen on the streets. They tested positive for COVID-19. It might have been a mere coincidence!" I tried to defend Mili for some unknown reason.

"Oh well. We ladies are saying that if you see your face on the sidewalk, get yourself tested!" she said and laughed loudly at her own sarcastic joke.

I didn't believe Mrs. Smith. At least not that night.

Soon it became the talk of the whole neighborhood as more and more ended up on the sidewalk scribbles, and then at the mortuary. I still found it difficult to comprehend that people were willing to believe that a five-year-old girl was capable of such demonic power.

I had a different theory. I felt that the virus was silently taking over the minds of the people, making them hallucinate their deepest fears, something that probably the world was still not aware of. I didn't have a medical degree to back up my thoughts. So, I decided to go and check her sketch the next morning to see if there was any ounce of truth in the neighborhood rumor.

I covered my face with a mask and wore a pair of gloves. I didn't take Simba with me because I thought I would do a quick jog and be back in a few minutes. I saw Mili at her usual place, drawing with no care in the world. She had covered her face with a mask too, and her hair had grown longer than what I had seen in the past. It touched her shoulders now.

I waved at her as she looked up.

"Hello, sunshine!!" I said.

I crossed the street and looked at her drawing. She had sketched Sana and a tall guy next to her who must have been Jai.

I stood there frozen not sure what I should do; I felt my rationale slipping through the cracks of the sidewalk and being replaced by the facts of the rumor.

I started to question things that I had never questioned before.

Why had she never drawn her parents before? Why now?

That was the last time I saw Mili. A few days later, I saw an ambulance standing outside their house while I was walking my dog. I couldn't bring myself to go and check what was happening, given the way the virus was spreading in my area. I thought of checking with them later, but I haven't seen the whole family ever since.

No one ended up on the sidewalks ever again, but a lot of people continued with their journey to the grave.

Mr. Anderson, Mrs. Anderson, Mrs. Desai, Mr. Walker, Mr. Hunt, Mr. Martinez, Sana, Jai, Mrs. Smith, Rene...

Eventually everyone in my locality started to blame the real culprit instead of hiding behind a child's art.

But some nights I still wonder if Mili is out there, and does she draw faces on the sidewalks?

MIRROR, MIRROR ON THE WALL

ADI NARESH

*A*di stared at his reflection in the bronze mirror. His face appeared to have thinned, making his cheekbones more prominent. He had dark circles around his brown eyes, which made him look like a sleep-deprived maniac. Despite his pale skin and handsome features, there was something about that face that made him look all worn out. He couldn't recognize his own reflection these days. He was so lost in his thoughts that he didn't even realize that Siya was standing right behind him. Her gaze was steady, and her wheatish complexion looked vibrant in the metallic sheen of the bronze mirror.

"When did you come to my study?" he asked a little startled.

"I have the results," Siya said.

Adi nodded silently. He had been waiting for the results for a long time.

"What does it say?" he asked.

"You don't have schizophrenia. Your wife and therapist are in this together. They are all lying to you. They want you dead so that they can take all your wealth and property," Siya said nonchalantly. There was no expression in her strikingly beautiful face. But Adi could sense a feeling of betrayal in her voice. She sounded distant yet concerned at the same time.

Adi stared at Siya's reflection without turning back to look at her, trying to register what she had just said. He knew deep in his heart that Siya would only confirm his darkest fears. Siya was his only friend at this point. Although he didn't exactly remember when he had first met her, he always thought it was during one of the parties that his wife used to throw in her art gallery. But in the last year, Siya had become his good friend and an only confidante. His wife hardly understood his state of mind, and instead thought that he was psychotic. Siya was there all the time to hold his hand. Even when the world looked at him with doubt and pity, Siya stood by him like a rock. It was not her flawless skin or startling blue eyes that he found attractive; instead, it was her silence and steadfast belief in him that bonded him to Siya.

"These medicines that they gave you, will slowly kill you," Siya said after a long pause.

Adi was annoyed with himself for taking so long to believe this conspiracy that his wife had carefully hatched. He could feel his frustration building up. Like a good husband, he always gave his wife the benefit of doubt, even when his guts screamed hatred toward her. He even went to the therapist every day, thinking something might be wrong with him, only to realize that his wife was trying to get him killed through those therapy drugs! It was difficult for him to believe that his wife and the old shrink were in this together. She had already proved to everyone in his family and workplace that he was some sort of a lunatic with crazy hallucinations, but the fact that she would go to the extent of taking his life was something he was still having a hard time believing. He had to stop her somehow.

"What do I do, Siya? How could my wife do such a thing!" Adi said as he knelt, unable to shoulder his emotions.

He hid his face in his arms and let the tears roll down. He didn't care that Siya had to witness his emotional side. He wanted to stop all this nuisance, once and for all.

"I would have killed her. After all, survival of the fittest," Siya said. Her ice-cold voice cut through him like a knife in cheese. It was the harsh truth, and Siya always spoke her mind. That was another thing he liked about her.

Before Adi could raise his head and react to her, Siya was already gone. She was always quick with her exits. One time she would be there and the next moment she would just disappear. Adi never questioned that about Siya though. At least she was there for him when he needed her.

He could now hear the jingle of the keys at the front door.

It was his wife, Maya. She was home.

He had met his wife five years ago when she was trying to open an art gallery called Jhanak Boutique in the heart of South Mumbai to sell antiques. He had found her charismatic and quite attractive and her ideas futuristic. He knew how rich people were always enamored with artistic and indigenous things so, deep in his heart, he could see it becoming a growing business. He ended up investing a huge part of his money in her gallery. It became a huge hit, and he prided in her accomplishments. But over the next few years, her greed consumed her so much that he felt she started to care more about his wealth and less about him. He always tried to ignore her late-night parties and art gallery expenses, but one night he lost his temper and hit her. He felt guilty the next morning to have raised his hand on her, and so, when she convinced him to see a therapist, he readily agreed.

Anything to make our relationship work. That was his only thought.

But then came the doctor's diagnosis of schizophrenia, and it escalated to a big family drama. Everyone slowly turned their backs on him, and he ended up spending most of his time alone in his study room. That was the only place where he felt safe and comfortable.

His study was a small room on the east side of their huge apartment in Juhu. It even had a balcony of its own, overlooking the visitor parking lot. He had designed the interiors of this study, and that's probably why he felt more at home here. The only thing in this study that reminded him of his wife was the bronze mirror, which he had bought from her gallery at some charity auction last year.

"Adi, are you back?" Maya called, breaking his train of thoughts.

Adi grunted back in response. He didn't want to look at her or talk to her and hoped that his response would suffice and she wouldn't come to the study room looking for him.

"There you are. How was your therapy session?" Maya asked as she entered the study.

She was wearing a long black gown that highlighted her petite figure. She was still attractive, but now that Adi knew about her true self, he was disgusted with her.

"What do you care? Stop acting like anything matters to you!" Adi said, losing his patience. He couldn't go around pretending anymore.

"Adi, did you take your medicine?" Maya asked, her tone suddenly changing.

He didn't like it when she spoke to him like that. He was not some nut job who would need to be babied. He knew where this conversation would go. If he said no, she would hand the medicine to him and look at him with those doe eyes of hers, which would melt his heart and he would end up taking them.

But not today, he told himself.

He grabbed the bottle of pills that were lying on his study table and walked toward the open balcony in fury . He mockingly gestured the bottle toward Maya's confused face before throwing it down from the 18th floor. Maya came running behind him trying to stop him, but it was too late.

"You thought you could kill me…Now watch me kill you!!" Adi suddenly pulled her by her arms and whisked her hard so that her face was inches away from his. Her eyes portrayed horror. For the first time, she looked scared and that's exactly what Adi wanted to see.

She tried to push him away with her other hand, but he tightened his grip on her arm instinctively, and she squealed in pain.

"Leave me, Adi! You are hurting me!"

"What about the pain you inflicted on me? That's justified?" he scoffed.

Adi thought it felt good to see her squirm. He couldn't believe that he had loved this woman so much, but he reminded himself that it was she who had brought out his demonic side, and tonight she would have to die because of that. He still didn't know how he wanted to kill her, but even though he could feel his blood boil in anger, he didn't want to cause her pain.

It must be sudden and painless, he told himself.

He suddenly loosened his grip and walked back inside. His heart felt heavy, and he could feel his hands shaking a bit. He looked around with uncertainty. All he could see around his study were books, the table, and his leather chair. There was nothing in there that could kill someone.

He could hear Maya sobbing and saying her usual things to calm him down, but he tuned her out. She always did this, and he would always give in to her sweet hypnotic voice and tears.

But tonight, I have a plan. Enough of this lying, he told himself.

I would have killed her. He could still hear Siya's voice resonate in his ears. It almost felt like she was right next to him. He turned his face hoping to see her face, but instead saw the bronze mirror. He could see Maya and the balcony door in its reflection, and he immediately pulled the mirror from the wall. It was heavy and it had spikes all around it, and that's exactly what he needed.

He balanced it between his two hands and turned to face Maya one last time. Adi was standing right opposite to the balcony door, and he could see Maya still standing on the balcony, soothe talking to him. She looked confused as he stood there facing her with the mirror in his hands.

"Adi, put the mirror down…you will break it! It's an antique…" Maya's voice trailed as Adi ran toward her, screaming like a mad man.

He was going to push those metal spikes into her and watch her fall down the eighteen floors to her much deserved fate. *You love this mirror so much, so take it and leave,* he thought wryly.

Maya stood frozen, gaping at him wide-eyed.

He was just inches away from her when suddenly she swerved to the right. It was too late for him to change his course. He tipped over the short railing balcony that he had specially designed for this room. His design became the reason for his fall. His eyes widened in shock as his hands gripped the mirror tightly. He gasped for air, and his mouth dried up as he fell. Everything was a blur, a blur that swirled out of existence. Suspended in midair, he closed his eyes and surrendered himself to those blue eyes as the finality of the moment hit him.

MAYA NARESH

She shrieked in horror, hands over her mouth, completely bewildered as she stood there on the balcony, still as a statue. Her face was stuck in an incredulous expression, white as chalk and her head whirled in disbelief at what had just happened. Her brain desperately scrambled to make sense of it all as she stood there speechless and incapacitated. She could see people starting to gather around the corpse of her husband, but she didn't know what to do. She couldn't even fathom if her husband was trying to kill himself or if he was trying to kill her or if all this was just a result of some hallucination he was having.

Suddenly, the cold air hit her face, and she staggered back in the study looking for her phone.

I need to call the police and an ambulance.

She waited impatiently for the sounds of the emergency vehicle as she walked down the stairs to check on Adi. She always preferred taking stairs specially when things weighed in on her mind. Her brain was hardly functioning well, and the never-ending staircase somehow seemed to calm her down a bit. She hesitated a bit as she stepped down the last stair.

I must be strong, she told herself.

She drew a deep breath and walked toward Adi. People made way for her the moment they saw her. Someone held her shoulders while others whispered some words that didn't hold any meaning for her. They all blended into some nameless face, even though she knew most of the people standing there. They were once her friends and neighbors, but today she was here to see her husband one last time, and everyone else could wait.

She broke down the moment she saw his bloodied body clutching the mirror.

He was, after all, the love of her life, and it came as a shock when the doctor had diagnosed him with schizophrenia. The last year of their marriage was the most confusing and trying time for her. He lost his job soon after his diagnosis, and his mom died of a heart attack a few months after, unable to cope with the fact that her son had mental health issues. She was the only one Adi had, and she tried her best to be there for him.

Now as she stood there all alone, the bottled-up emotions burst out of her in the form of tears. She sobbed and tears flooded like the waters rushing down from a waterfall. The only time she'd stop was to fill her lungs with fresh air, and then the sobbing would start again.

The next few days went in a haze. The police took his body for forensics, which confirmed death from a fall. Adi's therapist confirmed that such cases with schizophrenics were quite natural. When they, at last, returned the body, it was all frozen and the blood had dried up. She couldn't even recognize the cold body that lay in front of her. She, like a robot, performed all the rituals that were expected of her. People swarmed in her home like ants, and she saw them coming in and going out, but for her everything was gray and foggy, just like her emotions. She moved around the house like a silhouette of herself, feeling all mangled. She wanted all of this to end soon so that she could grieve alone in silence.

When at last the day arrived when everyone left, she sat down in Adi's study and cried for hours. Every memory played like a song in her head.

She still vividly remembered how it had all started with his erratic mood swings. One day he would be his normal self, but the very next day he would surprise her with some crazy things. He had once told her that their maid was threatening him for money, and Maya couldn't understand what had triggered such allegations. In the end, she believed him because he was the one who stayed home the whole day. Another time, Adi had even claimed that he had invested in her art gallery and when Maya denied any such thing, Adi had gotten furious and called her a gold digger. She wondered whether she should have taken him seriously then and got him some help right away, and then maybe he would have lived to see the light of the day today. But she let her love for him blind her, and such kind of behavior continued. He would scream in his sleep, talk alone in his study, and even have long conversations with his reflection in the mirror. None of it made sense to Maya, but she reasoned it in her head that it was a phase and it would go away when his stress reduced. He was, after all, a well-known book editor, and she thought that it was his work tension that was making him whimsical. She blamed herself now for not acting on it soon enough and for letting Adi build a crazy version of the real story.

After a long time, she dried her tears and opened the doors of the balcony to let in the fresh air. The sun had long set behind the horizon, and what lay before her was the impending darkness, waiting to engulf her in sadness. She decided to clean his study, which was strewn with books and papers. Cleaning always helped her to focus her thoughts better, while her mind tried to comprehend the fact that her Adi was gone forever now. Her hand traced his face on a photograph of theirs on the study table. They used to be happy together, and she wanted to have that as the last memory of him.

She still remembered the day they had both met. She had just inaugurated her gallery, and he had walked in on the launch party uninvited. He was a struggling editor back then, and free food was all he cared for. His office was right next to hers, and when the security informed her of his trespassing, she let him be because something about him caught her eye. He was not a cheap guy eating her food. He looked genuine and handsome. She wanted to know him better, and that's how it all started. Luckily for him, his struggles ended soon, and he bagged a stable job as a book editor in a well-paying firm. The photograph on his desk was from the first trip they took with his salary to Manali. That was a trip he financed with his first salary as an editor. She smiled at this thought.

She continued to arrange the papers at his desk. There was an unopened envelope lying on his desk marked *Results*. She opened it wondering if there were some new results from the therapist's office that she had missed. But all she found inside was a blank paper inside scribbled with words: *"They are going to kill you."* She threw it in the trash can, shaking her head. This had Adi written all over it.

Suddenly, her eyes caught a diary lying at the bottom of the trash can. She hadn't seen that before, so she picked it up and went through the pages.

It was filled with scribbles, gibberish, and numbers that didn't make any sense.

> *I feel that I am getting worse.*
> *Maya doesn't understand me.*
> *Someone is trying to kill me.*

Dr. Pati is a lunatic fool.
Abgdai aluewoqu hahoeuwro
ADJ - 8497
I love you, Siya.

The last words caught her attention. Just below it was a pen sketch of a hauntingly beautiful pair of eyes. It felt so real that Maya closed the diary immediately. She looked around the study a little more and found Siya scribbled in different places—books, papers, and whatnot.

Weirdly, the name sounded familiar to her, and like a flash, she remembered that Dr. Pati, the therapist, had mentioned this name before. She threw the diary back in the trash can and dialed Dr. Pati's number. Her grief was suddenly replaced with an uncertain anxiety.

The next day she found herself face-to-face with Dr. Pati. He was an old man, and she had met him so many times in the last year that he had almost become a family. He knew everything that Adi was going through and the trauma that Maya had to bear with as a caregiver.

"I am so sorry to hear about Adi…It was very unfortunate," Dr. Pati said.

Maya nodded, not knowing how to ask the real question for which she had come.

Dr. Pati continued when he saw no response from Maya.

"Adi had built a world around himself. He had his own version to everything. Like he thought, he was a successful editor all his life and everyone, including you, were after his money. He didn't even remember that his mother had expired and instead believed that you turned his family against him. All these hallucinations must have triggered some intense emotion within him, that he must have jumped from the balcony to end it all. So, don't be hard on yourself, Maya. There was nothing you could have done to prevent this," he said.

"Actually …I wanted to ask you something else," Maya said a little hesitantly. "You had once asked me about Siya… That was right…when he started the therapy with you…Umm…Did Adi talk about her after that?"

"Yes. He always spoke highly about her. I remember it well because she was the only thing that sounded very real. Everything else that he used to talk about, like his fears, paranoia, hallucinations, etc. would change daily. But you and Siya always remained constant," Dr. Pati said.

"Umm…Can you please tell me honestly, Dr. Pati… Did you at any point think he was having an affair with Siya?" Maya asked, dreading what he might answer. That was the only question weighing heavy on her, more than the grief of losing Adi at this point.

Dr. Pati smiled and patted her hands.

"I don't know about an affair, Maya." Dr. Pati sighed and paused momentarily. "But if you ask me if she was real or his hallucination. I would say Siya was real…But look, Maya, Adi is dead and I feel like you should move on too instead of burdening yourself with such things."

Maya sat there feeling numb and frozen.

Dr. Pati shuffled a few papers on his desk and pulled something out while Maya closed her eyes trying to wrap her head around what she had just heard.

"By the way, Maya," Dr. Pati continued. "I have been meaning to tell you that some of the family results came back last week, and I noticed that even your family has a history of schizophrenia. I think we should talk about that…I am a little worried about you…"

Maya stared at Dr. Pati blankly. Nothing else mattered to her right now.

Before Dr. Pati could finish his statement, Maya walked out of his office because she felt a wave of emotion suddenly grip her. Dr. Pati's belief that Siya was real confirmed her fears that Adi was having an affair after all. She couldn't believe that Adi would do this to her.

Their relationship was not the same after his diagnosis, and Maya wondered when he could have met Siya. He rarely stepped out of the house.

Did he meet Siya in the waiting room of the therapist? Is that why Dr. Pati said that Siya was real?

All kinds of thoughts flooded her mind, and for a change, she cried tears of anger. She couldn't even bring herself to go back to the apartment. More than Adi, it somehow started to echo of Siya, and she didn't want to deal with that insecurity and the feeling of disgust anymore. She decided to crash at her friend's place for the week while she dealt with her newfound emotions.

Over the next few days, Maya immersed herself in work, trying to forget the last five years of her life. It was not easy, and most days she was burdened with excruciating pain that mired her thoughts. The misery of his absence still haunted her, but the viciousness of his betrayal shattered her from within. To make matters worse, the police arrived one evening at her art gallery with the bronze mirror—the mirror Adi had jumped with. It immediately brought back every memory that she had stopped her mind from revisiting.

"Ma'am, we didn't find you at your apartment, so we came to drop this here," Inspector Mathur said. "The case has been closed. So, you can have this back"

She nodded as she watched them place the mirror against the wall. She would have preferred if the mirror like any other mirror had shattered during the fall. But it was a mirror completely made of bronze and to her dismay, it had survived the eighteen-floor fall with no damage. The only thing that got shattered in all this was her marriage and her belief in love.

Maya struggled to keep her emotions in check. She touched the mirror with her fingers. There were still traces of Adi's blood around the edges. This was not just any mirror. It was an antique mirror from the fifteenth century that Maya had bought from a dealer in Hampi for her art gallery. Its front surface was made of bronze, but it was polished to look all shiny, whereas the back was the usual metal with ornate designs all around it. When light reflected on the polished surface, its surface became transparent just like any other mirror and she could see her reflection. Around the circular rim, it had metal shaped like the sun's rays. When hung in a bright room, it would look like a small sun, but that evening, as she stared at it, it just gleamed a little in the dimly lit gallery. She noticed that one of the metal-shaped rays had become loose, probably because of the fall. She pulled it out, wanting to glue it back on.

As she looked for the glue, her mind wandered to the night, how by mistake the package containing the mirror was delivered at her home address, and how consumed Adi was with it. He had never shown any interest in any of the artwork Maya had, and she had been pleasantly surprised when she found him staring and touching the mirror, charmed by its uniqueness. So, when Adi had asked her that night if he could keep it in his study, she couldn't say no. Adi meant the world to her, and the gallery could do without one piece of art, that was her reasoning. But it was pretty much after that night that her life started to crumble. She didn't realize it before, but this was the last happy memory she had of them together before schizophrenia and Siya happened. Later, this reality was torn apart, as Adi replaced the truth with his own version. Some days he believed that he had bought it from her art gallery, while some other days he believed that Maya was spying on him through the mirror. She could see what Dr. Pati was trying to tell her the other day. His hallucinations told him different things all the time, *but you and Siya always remained constant.*

The thought of Siya suddenly evoked disgust within her. The pain of Adi's loss vanished and replaced itself with a fire seed in her belly. Siya still haunted her dreams. Most days, she managed not to think of her, but looking at the mirror suddenly, all she could think of was Siya and the betrayal that she was left with after Adi's demise. The happiness in her life had been all sucked out, and she felt lonelier than ever.

She threw the broken metal piece that she was holding and was about to pick up the heavy mirror to throw it out, when something caught her eye. It was not her reflection in the mirror that made her jump. It was the heavenly blue eyes of a damsel that stared at her from the mirror. She wanted to look away, but she couldn't. There was something weird happening to her senses. Maya felt like she was drifting away. She had been so consumed with Siya and Adi's betrayal, that for a second, she thought she had started to hallucinate.

"Mayaaaa…We meet at last," said a sonorous voice.

"Who a-are y-y-you?" Maya could barely whisper the words.

"Weren't you looking for me? Well…here I am…the infamous Siya"

Maya continued to stare at the doe-eyed woman. She could feel her reality slip through her fingers. Suddenly, nothing else mattered to her anymore. She didn't even know why she was looking for Siya. All that mattered were those blue eyes and her voice. That was her reality now.

The next day, Maya was found dead inside her gallery. There were no traces of violence. She had cleanly slit her wrist with a metal piece, which looked to be a broken part of the mirror. She was found lying arms outstretched next to the bronze mirror. There was blood splattered on the mirror, and the police took the mirror back again to the station for further investigation.

"If only the mirror could talk, we would know why these two died!" Inspector Mathur joked as his men loaded the mirror into the police van.

THE DARK KINGDOM

The train slowed down as it entered the city of Varanasi. Some said that this city was older than the legends, filled with myths and mysteries, and served as an allegory between life and death. But Mrs. Rajni Devi was detached to all things associated with this place. For her, this was her usual annual travel destination from Patna, just to meet her only son, Kedar. He had moved to Delhi after finishing his college, and since then the mother and son duo had started a new tradition. Every year they would spend a week together in the streets of Varanasi, away from their reality and basking in the glory of the unknown. This city always inspired Kedar to film every moment through his photographic lens, and Rajni loved being in cahoots with her son's whimsical ideas. She had, after all, reached that stage in her life wherein her happiness was just a mere reflection of her son's desires.

She limped her way out of the train, and her poor vision searched for a familiar face amidst the teeming crowd—black hair, tall and slender figure with brown eyes that shone like diamonds. It was a face like everyone else, yet unique and like no other. Out of nowhere, Kedar hugged Rajni, and the shadows of their reunion stretched long in the setting sun.

Every year, Rajni would look at her son and exclaim, "You have grown so thin! I need to find a girl for you soon," and every year, Kedar would laugh it off, reckoning how could the solution for everything be in marriage. But that's how it would always begin— their therapeutic journey amidst the chaotic streets of Varanasi. A city named after the two rivers, Varanā and Asi.

They wandered through the timeless alleys of Varanasi as if it were their first time in this city. The dim orgy of the setting sun mingled with the smoke of the burning sandalwood to create a trance-like realm wherein anyone could easily drift to a different time, a time dating back to 3,000 years when the never-ending cacophony of the crowds easily blended with the spiritual temple bells! Kedar pulled out his camera to seize this fleeting moment, but what his camera captured was a smoky-hued crowded labyrinth instead.

"Always look and feel through your eyes; lenses can lie but eyes don't," Rajni said as Kedar rolled his eyes.

He was used to such words of wisdom from his mother. It was like a daily dose of some moral medicine that Kedar had now grown immune to. As they walked through the streets lost in their thoughts, Rajni suddenly spotted a beautiful temple, hidden behind some trees.

"Let's go there. It looks pristine, and by the sound of it, the evening rituals must be going on too!" Rajni exclaimed.

Rajni pointed in the direction of a small dome-like ancient structure, lit with several candles and reverberating with rhythmic hymns. Kedar hesitated a little. He was looking forward to the daily evening rituals at one of the Ghats[1]. But then he spotted the dim sparkle in Rajni's eyes, and something within him smiled at her childlike desire. He just couldn't say no to that.

He and Rajni stood at the temple entrance with folded hands, and although the religious ceremony at the temple looked mesmerizing to the unaccustomed eyes, Kedar was looking for something artistic to capture through his lens. He had taken a photography course in the last month, and his heart ached to try those new strategies.

"Mom, can you attend this alone? I am going to walk a little and come back in a few minutes," Kedar whispered.

Rajni was lost in the hypnotic charm of the dancing lights, tinkling bells, and the aromatic smell of burning incense, so she just nodded slightly.

Kedar stepped onto the streets looking for the right kind of photographic stooge. He captured a cat hiding beneath some flower garlands, and then moved on to a lady cleaning cow dung from outside her shop, but all these pictures were missing the true spirit of the city. He continued to look for that quintessential piece that would complete his photographic pilgrimage.

Through his lens, somewhere in the corner of the street, he spotted a sage, popularly known as an *Aghori*[2], sitting under a gigantic Peepal[3] tree. He had seen and heard a lot about them. Social media had made *Aghori* saints symbolic to Varanasi.

A perfect picture of an Aghori would surely complete my Varanasi portfolio, Kedar thought.

He fumbled through his pocket for some cash as he made his way toward the *Aghori*. He had recently read an article that had unmasked the truth behind these ash-faced saints that pervaded the streets of this holy city. According to the journalist, all these *Aghori* were nothing but actors who dressed up and roamed in the streets of Varanasi. Their technique was simple: *Give money. Take photo*. The author had argued that these *Aghori* were homeless people who had found an easy way to make money, as all tourists wanted to get pictures of the *Aghori*. After all, what's Varanasi without an *Aghori* in the frame? Most people believed that the real ones lived high up in the mountains of the Himalayas, and they rarely came down to the cities. Kedar, for some unknown reasons, had loved that article. He had found it fascinating—the journey from being homeless to fake paid characters sounded as mythical as this place could get.

As he neared the tree, he felt his heart thump a little. A voice at the back of his head screamed in fear, *What if it's a real Aghori?*

He knew the reason behind his trepidation. A real *Aghori* was one of the most feared and revered shamans who were associated with post-death rituals, cremation, and were infamous for their ascetic ways of living and cannibalism. People said that they had powers from beyond the grave. One look from them and you could cease to exist!

Sweat dripped into his eyes as he neared the *Aghori*. Kedar looked through his lens and wondered if he could stay far and still get a good shot. That would not only save his cash but also protect him from some unforeseen curse if he was a real *Aghori*.

The camera focused on the ash-covered, stark naked body that glistened blue in the twilight cast. His white beard intertwined with his messy hair, and everything about him seem to blur into one blob of flesh. The *Aghori's* eyes were scanning a young boy who sat right opposite him; both looked to be unaware of Kedar's presence. Kedar silently clicked the shutter.

The *Aghori's* voice at that precise moment echoed loudly.

"I see a great future for you, son. You will take pictures and travel the world. Your brilliance will shine through"

For a split second, Kedar thought that the *Aghori* was talking about him instead of the boy. He felt his hair raise a bit, and a cold shiver ran down his spine. He shook that feeling off with a rational thought.

The Aghori must have seen me with a camera, and he used the common trick any fortune teller would use to fool their audience.

That thought completely calmed Kedar. He believed it in his mind that the saint was a fake one. He stood in the shadows of the street as he watched the little boy scramble back to his feet. From the distance where Kedar stood, it looked like the boy dropped some money into the skull bowl that the *Aghori* was holding in one of his hands.

Whatever tinge of doubt Kedar had, dispersed instantly. He knew what he had to do to get a picture of the *Aghori*. Kedar wanted to be in a controlling position so that he was not duped by some home-less man. In India, being soft and docile was always thought to be a sign of weakness. Either you took the position of command or you ended up chafing under the command of someone else. Kedar didn't want to end up being the latter, so he squared his shoulders and walked toward him with a renewed sense of authority. All his lost courage returned with full vigor as he pulled out the cash from his pocket.

"This should be enough for taking a couple of pictures of you," Kedar said as he handed a wrinkled 100 rupees note to the ascetic.

The *Aghori* who looked to be meditating, slowly opened his eyes. He looked at the damp currency note on Kedar's hand and smiled serenely.

"What do you *really* want, my boy?" he asked.

"I just want to take a picture of you," Kedar retorted.

"Didn't you already take some from that corner?" The *Aghori* raised his frail hand and pointed in the direction where Kedar stood a minute before.

"So, you *did* see me!" Kedar said. "I also saw you pull that trick with that little boy," he added.

"So, you believe what I did was a trick?"

Kedar shrugged. He couldn't understand why he was being asked so many questions.

Things I must do to get a picture these days, Kedar thought. To humor the ascetic, Kedar continued with the charade while trying to focus his lens.

"Umm...What has my belief got to do with anything? I just want to take couple of pictures of you," Kedar said after a brief pause.

"Well…" The *Aghori* momentarily paused, but his eyes twinkled a little as he continued. "Your belief is everything, son. What you believe, isn't that the sole truth for you?"

Kedar frowned a little, contemplating what the *Aghori* just said. There was some ounce of weight in his talks. Although Kedar didn't know the answer to his question, he couldn't disagree that the sage appeared to be quite prudent.

A learned homeless he must be, he thought silently.

Somewhere deep within him, his heart twitched a little and warned him not to go too far with this, but his inquisitive instincts got the better of him.

"What do you mean?" Kedar asked.

He closed his camera shutter because that no longer enticed him, and he sat right where the other boy was sitting. He wanted to hear what the *Aghori* had to say. He wanted to get to the bottom of this whole act.

Could he continue this charade forever? Kedar wondered.

But the *Aghori* continued to smile as if his question didn't bother him. "Think about it, son. When you believe in something with full force, its roots go so deep down your soul that no one else can tell you otherwise. That's the power of belief because it becomes the truth for you."

"I don't agree with you. What if I believe in something but it's not the truth?" Kedar suggested.

"Hmmm…. You tell me, my boy. Will your belief change then?"

The *Aghori* noticed the confusion spread across Kedar's face like an inkblot.

"Let me show you something. Give me your palms," the *Aghori* suddenly commanded.

Their positions had been swapped, but Kedar was so bemused by him that he gladly obliged. His curiosity got the best of him, and he tuned out his nagging fears. The frail fingers of the *Aghori* gently traced the lines in his palms. Kedar gazed at the *Aghori* as if he were connected to the ascetic by an invisible bond.

Is it some divine charisma or some tantric hypnotism? Kedar wondered silently.

I think he is a real Aghori. Kedar heard a faint voice in his head.

But he doesn't look angry at all. He probably wants more money, so he is weaving this whole queer act. His mind reasoned immediately to shun that voice.

He had seen in the past too that sometimes the actors get so attached to their characters that it becomes difficult for the viewers to understand the difference.

This guy is good in the art of acting! he thought.

The *Aghori* continued to stare at his palm for several minutes. He then closed his eyes, and his lips moved in silent chants. Kedar waited for something exciting to happen, but minutes passed, and nothing happened. After a while, he started to lose his interest in the whole palm-reading act. The *Aghori* had been sitting motionless for quite some time now, and Kedar felt stupid to sit there with open palms. He looked around and realized that it was starting to get dark already.

He called out to the *Aghori* several times, but there was no response from him either. He found that weird, but then he figured there was probably no more wit left in the *Aghori* to carry on this conversation, so he had ended it abruptly.

This is a poor end to the show, but then again, it is the Aghori's show, so he has to play it by his rules, Kedar thought.

He decided to take a couple of pictures of the contemplative *Aghori* and call it a day. He dropped the crumpled note into the skull bowl once he was done with his photography and started to walk out.

But suddenly from behind, the voice of the Aghori bellowed in a deep surreal manner:

> *"You think you know it all, son*
> *But life is full of mysteries, you see.*
> *So, I give you this coin that holds your future*

It will define what your life will be.
Learn to balance your head and heart
For those two will keep you sane
Head rules most times
But heart knows when reality wanes.
I give you this advice
But life is what you weave,
You are the master of your fate
So, your fortune depends on what you believe."

Kedar looked back, unsure with the turn of events, but the *Aghori* seemed to be in a trance. The blacks of his eyes were rolled back, and the white flashed brightly. He even felt the wind pick up speed, and a definite howl could be heard. He also noticed fumes coming from the skull bowl where he had dropped the money a few seconds back. The *Aghori's* frail outstretched hand glowed in the dim light of the street, and Kedar could see a coin in his palm.

"That's some good magic, man!" Kedar muttered as he mock-clapped the saint. His hands shook slightly from what he had witnessed, but he tried to rationalize his thoughts to get a grip on himself again.

Before his mind could process anything, his fingers had already picked up the coin from the *Aghori's* palm.

It was a 10-rupee coin.

He looked at the *Aghori*, but he had gone back to his meditative state, oblivious to Kedar's presence.

"This is weird," Kedar mumbled and shook his head to discard the scary vibe he had felt a minute back.

He walked out from that place a little shaken but thoroughly impressed with the *Aghori's* drama. He vaguely remembered the *Aghori's* last words and wondered silently what he could have tried to imply.

What if he is a real Aghori and he did some voodoo magic on the coin? His heart shuddered.

I think he was just doing an act. He started reciting a poem at the end. How lame is that! his mind sniggered.

As he neared the temple to pick up his mother, his mind had concluded by then, that all this was a good piece of entertainment.

It had all the elements to qualify as good drama. It's like a mythical Disneyland with fake characters, entertaining the people with some trivial magic, he thought.

He opened his sweaty palm and looked at the coin he was still holding.

What a joke! I gave him 100 rupees, and he gave me a coin in return. What is 10 rupees worth these days! I don't need charity.

He immediately dropped the coin when he spotted his mother amidst the crowd of devotees. The coin rolled down the street and was instead picked by a beggar, who thanked the almighty for his grace.

Later that night, Kedar told Rajni about his tryst with the *Aghori* over dinner.

Rajni was concerned with the turn of events. No matter what social media said about *Aghori*, she had high reverence for them.

"You should never show your palms to anyone. Some people have the power to take away your fate," Rajni said softly.

"You believe in such ignorant things, Mom?"

"There are many things beyond your understanding, but that doesn't mean they don't exist. Anyway, give me the coin he gave you"

"Uh…I threw that away. It was a joke. You really didn't think I would keep that coin! I don't need to keep such handouts, Mom."

"Kedar...don't utter such words. The false pride in your talk is starting to worry me!" Rajni whispered. She looked cold, and her face had lost all luster.

Kedar had never seen his mother in such a dreadful state. He couldn't understand what the big deal was about all this but decided to change the topic for good.

They spent the next few days roaming the streets of Varanasi as planned. But something had changed in Rajni's demeanor. She touched the feet of every *Aghori* she spotted and handed them food and money like a peace offering.

Rajni in her mind had decided to do penance for her son and hoped it would prevent any undue effects of her son's ignorance.

Even when she returned from Varanasi to Patna, Rajni continued to do all kinds of religious things as penance. Her mind yearned every day to talk to Kedar, and no matter how long they spoke, she always worried about him. She started to live a life of waiting for something inevitable to happen.

As months went by, she started to notice even the most subtle changes in Kedar's voice. It filled her heart with darkness with each passing day. It didn't surprise her when Kedar lost his job a few months later. She asked him to come back home immediately, but he wouldn't listen. She could feel the impending doom waiting to engulf her son, but she didn't know how to protect him.

One morning she woke up panic-stricken. She hadn't heard from Kedar for over a week, and a dreadful feeling lingered on her mind. She tried to call him several times, but there was no answer. She immediately decided to travel to Delhi to check on him. But when she reached Kedar's apartment in Delhi, the landlord informed her that he had vacated the room a few days back. Rajni froze, not knowing who else to go to. She didn't know anyone else in Delhi. Something within her told her that this was it. Her worst nightmare had come true. Rajni collapsed on the floor as if Kedar had died. Tears rolled down her cheeks, and she wailed in pain as if someone had stabbed her.

Eventually she did reach out to the Delhi police, but after a few months, they concluded their search because they couldn't find any trace of Kedar.

It has been a decade now, and you can still see on a beautiful summer evening Rajni sitting at the steps of different temples in Varanasi. Rajni never found

Kedar. But she still visits Varanasi every year to continue the tradition, in memory of her only son.

She has also taken to feeding a beggar now, the one she always finds sitting at the corner of the temple where she had witnessed a trance-like Aarti [4] the last time she was there with her son. The beggar is more unusual than all the others; he doesn't have any lines on his palms! Some even believe that if you look closely, you may notice that the beggar resembles Kedar. But then again, this is a mystical land where reality fades into beliefs, beliefs become myths, and myths become legends.

WHAT'S IN THE BOX?

*I*t started as a pang of hunger for popularity, but how was I to know what it would lead me into?

I don't even remember how or when this craving started, but ever since I stepped into the world of social media, I wanted to be an influencer. What more could you expect from a twenty-one-year-old, fresh-out-of-college, computer engineer who bagged a big-shot job in a dream company? Life was perfect for me, but I had that inner zest to do something more. Influencer was the right platform to have more power over everybody. Don't we all want to be *"that face"* the whole world wakes up to? Sounds creepy, right? But isn't that what we all do right now? The moment we wake up, we scroll through the endless list of applications on our phones, we subscribe to multiple channels in the social platform, buy books publicized by folks we like, visit places that they have visited, and do things that they are doing. It is like being a new-age web celebrity, and I did not see anything wrong with my desire for attaining that.

Probably because I come from a very traditional family, I wanted to do exactly opposite of what my upbringing was. My family had the flavors of Kolkata[1] written all over them. Although we braved the dark winters of Minnesota now, some days I could swear it felt exactly like I was right there among the chaotic residents of Kolkata. My parents moved to the United States years back, and I was born and brought up here in Minnesota. I have been to India several times, but that reduced as I grew up. I don't have much recollection of my roots anymore. For me, life in India is synonymous with whatever happens at my home in the name of tradition.

For instance, today my day will start at 4 a.m. As soon as the clock strikes four on an October new moon night, it will all begin. Birendra Krishna Bhadra's voice will echo as he recites the timeless *Mahisashur Mardini*—a tale of how Goddess Durga[2] arrived on Earth, and that will not only wake us up but probably the entire neighborhood. But from my past experiences, I knew that the only way to wake up at 4 a.m. was not to sleep the whole night. This has been my secret tradition, and I have always used these extra hours to do something fruitful. Tonight, I browsed through several YouTube videos looking for that one thing that would make me go viral. It was not until I ran across these popular videos that I realized the scope for my true potential—*Mystery Boxes from the Dark Web*. We lived, after all, in a world where the excitement of the unknown piqued our interests, and this was not just any unknown. It was right from the convoluted world of the deep dark web, and very few knew their way in and out of such perplexity.

As I looked through these videos, I realized that they had done an excellent job at creating that perfect eerie vibe. There was that uncanny, sinister music in the background, and what lay inside the boxes would vary in each video—from stolen goods to objects containing satanic imagery all over them. I could not understand why anyone would send you those items as a mystery box! But who am I to question, when the whole world was all gaga about it! I guessed that it must be the idea of some package coming from the uncharted territory, where only the most evil or the most adept could tread in, that made the prospect exciting for the viewers.

Weirdly, I was neither but still had the right tools and the knowledge to access it being a computer programmer. So, I decided to use my knowledge for a cause that could make me famous. It was a perfect night to bring out my inner Durga and make myself a celebrity. I am not exactly sure, but I think Durga was symbolic of this—she did something iconic and became a known and a worshipped celebrity.

I had been to the dark web several times, but I never quite understood the hush and the nonacceptance associated with this part of the web. People always connected dark web with drugs, weapons, smuggling, and prostitution. To some extent, it was true. After all, it couldn't be accessed by a normal browser, and all your activities in this digital netherworld remain untraceable. It was just like the normal web, only not orchestrated. You must be careful in there too, but the normal web was no different. These days scams happened everywhere. I even heard from my parents that scams happened long before the internet came in. I attribute it to human nature—the desire to trick people is wired in our brains, and whether it is the usual web or the dark one, people with this nature don't change. So, in my pea-sized brain, I correlated the dark web as a happening street; you stick to your lane and you will be fine. But if you venture into the unknown alleys, that's where things could get ugly and messy, and I knew my lanes very well here.

I threw a sly glance at the clock, which had 3:30 plastered on its face.

I still had some time.

I pulled up my laptop, which had the right configurations to get into the dark web. I easily jumped through a few hoops and circles, and before I knew it, I was in the unchartered ravines of the mysterious dark web. I could see a list of both legal and illegal items on sale in these markets, the obvious being guns and drugs. There were other kinds of things too: stolen credit cards to yearlong free Netflix accounts!

I ignored everything however tempting they looked.

I searched for "mystery box" and was shocked to see numerous options out there. I never knew they existed! People could shop here for mystery boxes as they did in other shopping sites. Bitcoin, litecoin, and monero were the only currencies you could use on the dark web, and luckily, I had just bought few bitcoins recently.

I looked through all kinds of weird options in there, and I noticed people bidding a lot of money on them. It was weird to see mystery boxes getting auctioned.

How can you bid for something when you don't even know what would come in it? What if it was an empty box they sent? Could it be a scam?

I was so immersed in my thoughts that I didn't realize that my mom was right outside my door. Hurriedly, I selected one of the options that had a lot of bids on it, and I typed in my home address.

My mom opened my door at that precise moment.

"Let's go!! It is going to start," she said.

My mom gave me a questionable look as she looked at my laptop screen that read:

You won the bid.

I had officially outbid all the other buyers.

That was quick! I thought.

"Are you gambling online?" my mom asked, trying to get a better look at my screen.

I slammed the laptop shut.

"No, Mom! Stop looking at my stuff!" I cried out.

"Gambling on a day like this! Haven't we taught you good things?" She started on her emotional black-mail speech.

"I was NOT gambling!! Can we go now?" I dragged her out of the door as she kept complaining about how I could get scammed and lose all my money. That was my mom—always thinking the world was out there to get us!

Due to all this racket, I didn't get a minute to reflect on the fact that I had ordered myself a mystery box —*a freaky surprise*. All I had to do now was wait and see. Perhaps, very soon, I would be a social media sensation!

As we watched the *Mahisashur Mardini* play on TV, my mind wandered to all kinds of things that I might be getting in the box. I didn't realize, but I dozed off to a beautiful dream where I had 10 million views on my creepy unboxing video.

But then a hard nudge woke me up. It was my mom again.

"Stop sleeping, Nisha. You are ruining the chastity of this whole thing."

I turned my sleepy head back to the television, which showed Durga with ten hands killing a demon, and the song soared to a high pitch to elaborate the victory of good over evil. As a child, watching this made a lot of sense, and it used to be fun back then, but I had long lost that interest because I discovered new nuances that kept my mind occupied. Like today I couldn't stop thinking of what I would find in my mystery box.

Will I be scared? Will my life change after that? I wondered silently as I watched the television.

Days turned into weeks, and my excitement slowly turned into concern. There was no sign of my mystery package anywhere. I was getting all my other packages delivered right on time from Amazon, but nothing like a mystery box was to be seen at my doorstep. To make matters worse, there was no package tracker on the dark web either where I could look up the package and see where it was stuck. I slowly began to fear that I had been scammed and lost all my bitcoins with which I had paid for it. I browsed through the deep dark web several times but couldn't bring myself to order another one.

It was definitely a scam.

Before I knew it, it was three months already and nothing had arrived. So, I decided to make a fake mystery box myself and do the video. The wait was just not worth it anymore. I went to a thrift store and picked up a box and filled it with some old books and clothes. I added a cracked picture frame and some creepy toys. On top of the box, I scribbled with red ink: SURPRISE!! Then I recorded my video in the garage for a dark theme and added a piece of chilling background music. With some sound and filter effects, it looked sensational. I uploaded the video and waited for my turn to go viral.

My friends thought that the video was good, but it was only they who thought that way, because I hardly got 100 views and 20 likes. My whole world came crashing around me. My dream to become an influencer looked far-fetched. I was so disheartened that I decided to stop dreaming about it and instead keep myself busy with my job. I never told anyone about my tryst with the dark web and my loss while ordering a mystery box. I didn't want to make a fool of myself any more than what I had already done.

I had almost forgotten about my venture into the dark web and the mystery package that I had ordered. To be honest, I didn't want to remember how foolish I had been in my quest for popularity. But one February morning, which happened to be my birthday, I heard my mom and dad arguing about a nameless package at our doorstep. I was not sure if this was it, but something made me run toward the door. I looked at the little brown-colored package that had a handwritten note on it which read: *Surprise!*

The package was hardly the size of a book—very different from the ones that I had seen on YouTube videos. I picked it up and traced my hands on the *Surprise* etched on it. It looked like it was freshly packed and not heavy at all. I didn't know for sure if it was the much-awaited mystery box, but I wanted to unravel its contents in my room, far from the curious, prying eyes of my parents. They looked at me suspiciously as I walked back to my room.

"It's my birthday gift. Nothing to worry about," I called out casually so that they wouldn't barge into my room while I opened it.

I could feel my heart thumping as I stepped into my room. I didn't have a boyfriend, so such a mysterious package on my birthday was totally out of question. I knew my friends well, and I knew exactly what they planned for my birthday. It didn't involve any packages. I stared at the handwriting that spelled *Surprise*. It was not a handwriting that I knew. It was a beautiful cursive, and l could have sworn that it was a girl. In my opinion, men wouldn't waste so much time to dot their *I's* and curl their letters.

Although I could feel my excitement beating like a drum, I couldn't bring myself to open the package at once. For a second, I thought of doing a recording of my unboxing. Wasn't that the whole intent of ordering from here? But I decided not to do a recording at this point after my fiasco the last time. Probably, once I saw the contents, I may have the heart to do a recording if it was worth it. Who knows, the box might be empty!

I slowly ripped off the tape and unwrapped the brown paper. Inside lay a thin black box. I opened the box, and there was a blue cashmere scarf. It looked beautiful, and I pulled it around my neck; it smelled of perfume, which meant it was a used scarf. I immediately took it off my body, slightly disgusted at the thought of it being a used item. For some unknown reason, I was reminded of those YouTube videos and the gruesome things that they unboxed. Who knows where this scarf was found? I kept the scarf on my bed while I pulled up the other contents of the box.

Inside it lay a turquoise clutch. It looked exquisite and yet vaguely familiar, but before I could dwell on it, I noticed a yellow card that lay just underneath the clutch. I pulled it up, and there was something written on it.

It was again that beautiful cursive that read:

"Your surprise is waiting for you in the car. Have a blast!"

I was completely intrigued and scared at the same time.

Both the items that I had pulled out so far looked to be used, but there was no story associated with them and luckily no blood either. I would be lying if I said I wasn't petrified at the thought of what I might find in my car, but I had to go and check it out.

I grabbed my car keys, scrambled out of my room, and ran toward the front door. My heart was still beating hard, and I felt faint in my knees with all the fear and excitement building up. After such a long wait, I had finally received my freaky surprise mystery box from the dark web. A part of me was just happy that I was not scammed. Was it worth the money? I wouldn't say so. But I kind of wanted to tell those YouTube video folks, "The dark web isn't what you guys show it to be. You just need to know your way, as I did."

I opened my front door and there was my car—1999 Red Solara—on the street, decorated with yellow balloons. I stood there for a long time, perplexed with the thought of how it all had happened. For a second, I wondered if this was all planned by my boring parents who had never ever planned a surprise for me. No, that thought was ridiculous! My head started to reel as I felt myself walk toward the car, as if being pulled by an invisible string.

I opened my car to check if there was anything else inside, and it looked clean—except for the fact that there was an envelope taped to my steering wheel. I was pretty sure I had locked my car last night when I got home from work. I pulled out the envelope, which had that same cursive writing on it.

"Happy Birthday, stranger! Hope you liked the freaky surprise!"

I opened the envelope and inside it was a picture of me sleeping in my bedroom. From the photo angle, it looked to have been taken from the door, and my face glowed clearly in the dim night light. Below it a note was written in the same handwriting:

"I love watching you sleep at night!"

My throat felt parched, and my blood ran cold. I stood there not knowing what else to do. I had heard of such horror stories happening on the dark web, but I always thought that it was to scare the novices away.

I ran back into the house, holding the photo to show it to my parents and to call 9-1-1 when I heard my mom complaining to my father.

"Look what your daughter did! I have been looking for this scarf and clutch for over a month, and she had it in her room all this time!"

My mom was holding the blue scarf and the sea-green clutch that had arrived in the package. I knew it was familiar, and now I know why!

There was no doubt that some intruders had gotten into our house and violated our privacy, but I had no idea how to break this news to my parents or the authorities. As I stood amidst it, panic ran up and down my spine. The note and the picture slipped from my hands. I felt my brain go fuzzy, and I slumped onto the floor.

It all started with a craving for fame, but it looks like I had found a sinister fan instead.

Here's the real *freaky surprise*: I have been receiving a package every week ever since. I don't open these packages anymore. The cops confiscate them as soon as they arrive. It has been a couple of months now, and they are still looking out for this suspicious person. There have been no leads so far. My family is even thinking of moving to a different house. I would prefer that too because I am scared to sleep at night.

Whoever said the dark web was innocuous...trust me they were all lying.

BURN APPÉTIT

*I*t was a dark, moonless night when the Hindu mythological deity, Lord Ram, the banished king of Ayodhya[1], returned home along with his wife, Sita. They had spent fourteen years in exile, and during that period he vanquished the ten-headed demon, Ravana, who had abducted Sita. To honor his victory and homecoming, the whole kingdom had lit their path with oil lamps. Thus, began the age-old tradition of decorating homes and public spaces with lights to mark the triumph of good over evil, and the five-day celebration came to be known as Diwali[2] in India. As time went by, this tradition transformed into a more fun-filled occasion for everyone to decorate their houses with rangoli[3], light firecrackers, and devour homemade sweets and salty snacks with extended family.

It was that time of the year again.

So, Lata pulled out her old-fashioned iron skillet to make her son's favorite Diwali sweet: coconut laddus. Laddus were Indian spherical balls made with lots of fat, sugar, and in this case with coconut as a base. It was not an easy recipe, but every year during this day, Lata always made sure that she made this delicacy for her only son, Neel. It warmed her heart when she watched him relish the laddus.

But beneath all this, was a lingering concern that she had for him. Every year during Diwali, somehow Neel always managed to get hurt. This had been going on ever since he was born. The first time it happened, Neel was hardly eleven months old then. He was crawling around the place, and in a moment of distraction from Lata's side, he ended up touching the hot wax of a candle. Luckily, it didn't burn his fingers that bad, but that's how the cursed phase began. No matter how much Lata tried to protect him, something inevitable would always happen during this festival. She shuddered a little at the thought of this.

As she stirred the coconut, she remembered how another time when Neel was around four, it was Lata's laddus that had burnt Neel's tongue. The thing with coconut laddus is that you have to turn it into spherical balls when the coconut is burning hot or else the ball disintegrates completely. Even Lata's palms would feel the pinch of the hot coconut while she molded them into balls. But her skin had hardened with years of practice and house chores. Neel, on the other hand, was a child, and being completely ignorant of how hot the laddus were, burnt his tongue when he swallowed one. Neel ended up standing in her kitchen open-mouthed, tongue burnt, and wailing in pain. She had immediately applied ice on his tongue, but the Diwali dinner was ruined that night. By the time she got back to her gas stove, the coconut had roasted completely, and dinner brewing in the other stoves were completely burnt. They ended up having curd rice that night with no alternative present. It was the most horrifying memory for Lata, and since then every time she cooked, she made sure Neel was never inside the house. Even today, she had asked her husband, Rana, to take Neel out for a stroll while she prepared dinner and sweets.

Such was Lata's misery. Every year, Diwali would laden her shoulders with unnecessary distress. While the world spent these five days in sheer exuberance, bereft of any stress, Lata spent sleepless nights worrying about Neel. Lata knew she was getting old, she didn't have the energy that she once had, and running after Neel was becoming more and more difficult for her. Neel had come in her life at a very late age. She and Rana had given up hope when Neel happened. It was a beautiful surprise, and she blamed herself for all of Neel's accident. She wanted to be a better mother and protect Neel forever.

She vividly remembered last year, when she had decided not to celebrate Diwali anymore. In retrospect, it was a lame attempt from her end to protect Neel. But Neel being his naughty self had run out of the house the first chance he got and fell on a lit fire-cracker. Luckily, only a couple of his fingers were burnt, and a visit to the emergency clinic sorted it out, but Lata suffered more watching Neel scream in pain. The doctors were kind enough not to doubt her parenting skills, but Lata hasn't been sure since then.

"Children always get hurt, Lata; you can't always protect them…That's how they learn to grow up!" the doctor at the emergency clinic had said when he saw her silent tears.

Lata nodded, but deep in her heart, she didn't agree. As a mother, her most important responsibility was to protect her son. *How can Neel get hurt with me around?* she wondered.

The only thing that bugged Lata more than her failure was the timing of the event. She couldn't understand why only during Diwali this would happen to Neel. All year round he would be fine, but something about this five-day festivity turned Neel into a complete klutz.

Tonight was the last night of the five-night festivity, and Lata was glad that in a few hours, it would be over. She could get back to her fretting the next year. Some days she wondered if Neel was cursed in some way.

She shook her head trying to dispel all these negative thoughts. She whispered a silent prayer to Lord Ram as she covered the laddus with a dry cloth.

Please, Lord...end this curse on Neel soon.

She suddenly realized that the heat from all the cooking was making her sweat profusely. It was November, but the humidity and heat in Mumbai hadn't reduced a bit. The hot flashes that she had developed lately because of her menopause added malady to her already agonized soul. She opened the kitchen window to let out the smoke. They lived in a small one-bedroom apartment in a populous society, and through the small kitchen window, she could see the busy street down below. There was a chaotic rhythm in the mundane trivialities. In the teeming crowd of cars, buses, and pedestrians, she spotted Rana. A smile blossomed on her hot red sweaty face.

They are back. But—

Her eyes immediately scanned the crowd, and her face clouded. Neel was nowhere to be seen. Lata felt the panic begin like a cluster of bees at the pit of her stomach. Her face and fingers froze on the kitchen windowsill, as she scoured to see that familiar face of her son—thin legs, short brown hair, and that bubbly face. Her breathing became more rapid and shallower while her mind played the incidents from the last six years. She felt suffocated. She could clearly see Rana now entering the gates of her apartment complex. He was holding a blue polythene bag, but Neel wasn't around. His shoulders looked hunched, which was never a good sign. Her heart hammered harder. The heat within her soared so much that she felt her skin burn. She sat on the cold floor so that her body and brain could cope, but darkness engulfed her.

Where is Neel, what happened, breathe, Neel is gone, no it can't be, Rana, are you home, what happened…(blackness)*…Where is Neel...*(creeping blackness)*...fire, I can't breathe, Neel...*(total darkness)*.

Lata opened her eyes, and the bright lights blinded her. She was lying on a hard bed, and her body still burned in pain. It was like some invisible flame was held against her skin. Rana, her husband, was standing at one corner of the room, still hunched. She didn't know where she was, but at that moment, it didn't seem to matter so much. She looked around to see if Neel was there.

"What happened, Rana?" another woman's voice echoed at the back of the room. "I was worried when I got your call!" she added. Lata couldn't catch a glimpse of the woman who had just walked in. Her back was turned towards her.

"Oh, Gita!" Rana sounded relieved. "Your sister's dementia kicked in again. She was fine when I went to the bakery downstairs. But…when I came back there was smoke in the whole house…and fire…and she is asking for Neel…" Rana's voiced trailed off.

"It's Diwali time…we should have known. Lata always worried about Neel during this time," Gita said as she held Rana's shoulders.

"B-b-but…How can she keep forgetting it every year that Neel is dead? It has been ten years now!! I can't do this anymore…" Rana sobbed harder.

"Let me talk to her," Gita said.

Gita pulled up a chair and sat beside Lata.

"Don't worry sis, I am here now!" she said softly as she held Lata's hand.

Lata pulled her hand away. She didn't know who this strange woman was and why she and Rana thought Neel was dead. She looked at Rana furiously instead and said in a hoarse voice, "Rana, can you just get Neel now? I don't want him to play with firecrackers. We have to protect him!"

"We can't, Lata…Neel died during the 1993 bomb blasts. We couldn't have protected him. He was coming back from college alone. Don't you remember?" Rana said with trembling lips.

Lata squinted her eyes as if recollecting the incident. She shuddered at the sudden sound of the firecrackers, which broke the silence of the room. She tried get herself up from the bed, but her body yelled in pain. Before she knew it, darkness engulfed her again.

LOCKED HEARTS

*R*itu was arranging the puffed pastry and egg rolls on the plate, but her mind wandered off a year back when she was dating Raj. The thought of that moment got her reminiscing about those charming days. They were both so young and naive back then, unaware of heartaches and pain. If someone had told her back then that they wouldn't end up together, she would have never believed them. They were perfect together, and their love burned with such fire that they believed they could leap over any walls or obliterate whatever obstacles. At least that's what she had thought until life made a fool of them. By a bitter twist of fortune and family drama, she ended up marrying a distant family friend, Anand, and never heard from Raj ever again. And just like that, her fairy-tale love story ended.

Anand became the new man in her life. He was nice, but reserved and distant. Also, since Ritu's parents never disclosed her past love history when she married him, she too, decided to never utter a word about it. After all, it was an arranged marriage, and she was not sure how open her husband would be about her past affair. *Some things are better left unsaid*, she thought, as many middle-class families still considered love affairs a big no-no. She settled into her new life, which was less about roses and dinner dates and more about mundane household chores, managing finances, and all things monotonous. Her only escape from all these humdrums was through her memories where Raj still lived on. She held on to her memories with Raj as long as she could, but then with time, he slowly became a figment of her obscured imagination.

Life was moving as planned for her. She had moved to a new city—far from the thoughts of her old town —made new friends, and that kept her mind away most days from thoughts of what her life could have been.

Bhoomi was her newfound bestie in this upscale neighborhood in Alipore, Kolkata. Her chatters were endless, and in spite of being preoccupied with life's unfairness, Ritu slowly warmed up to her company. In all these broken, conspired, and forced relationships, somehow Bhoomi became the only real thing. Bhoomi's husband worked late hours just like Ritu's, so these two girls ended up spending most of their time together, trying to fill the void with each other's presence.

Bhoomi peeked in the kitchen at that precise moment with a big flower vase in her hands.

"Are you done, Ritu? They will be here at any moment now!"

"Yeah …Stop worrying, Bhoomi…everything is ready!" Ritu muttered.

She hastily picked up the plate and followed Bhoomi into the living room trying to put a momentary pause on her thoughts.

Today, Bhoomi had arranged for a meeting with their society's president, Mrs. Sarkar, and one of her college friends Chirag. Their society was planning to celebrate their tenth housing anniversary next month, and Bhoomi being an active member in the society's board, suggested that they order food from *Chirag's Catering*. Chirag had a food catering service that the whole city was gaga about, and he had promised Bhoomi that he would give a huge discount.

"There's no business when it comes to friends… What's mine is yours!!" Those were Chirag's exact words to Bhoomi.

But Mrs. Sarkar wanted to meet the catering provider before making it official, and as always, Bhoomi decided to play the part of the perfect host.

Ritu didn't expect that Bhoomi would get her involved in this. But Bhoomi had gotten so used to their friendship that there was no way she would take no from her. Poor Bhoomi, she was completely unaware that all this was causing a series of panic attacks in Ritu's fluttering mind. It had been more than a year now, and Ritu hadn't thought about Raj so vividly until today. The truth was that her ex-boyfriend, Raj, used to be a silent partner in *Chirag's Catering*. Initially, when Bhoomi mentioned *Chirag's Catering*, Ritu's heart immediately skipped a beat. She reminisced about her golden days with him. Ritu couldn't help but wonder if their paths would ever cross again.

Will Raj come as well? Will I get to see Raj's face after all these months? Will he recognize me?

Ritu had agreed to help Bhoomi out without even thinking it through. Her lovelorn mind had conjured up all thoughts around Raj, and she didn't realize for a long time that it was Chirag who was coming to meet them, and not Raj. As her mind steadied a bit and reality hit her, a sudden wave of fright replaced her thoughts. She had never met Chirag personally, and she was not even sure if Raj had ever told him about their dating days. The only time Raj himself mentioned being an investor in this was when they passed by *Chirag's Catering* billboard on the highway. It was a very casual conversation, and they hardly went into the details of it. She had no idea how close

Raj and Chirag were, but there was no stopping her mind's trepidation.

What if Chirag knows about me and Raj? What if Chirag brings up something about Raj? What do I explain to Bhoomi then? What will Anand think if he gets to know about my past? How will all this affect my marriage?

All kinds of thoughts seethed in Ritu's mind as she walked into the living room with the puffed pastry egg roll platter. Her mind momentarily got distracted by the fact that Bhoomi had arranged for so many different items on the table that it didn't look like a gathering of four people, but instead, it looked to be a lavish house party. There was juice, chips, snacks, kebabs, and whatnot for an evening tea gathering. That was Bhoomi, always wanting to be in the front line when it came to social activities. Unfortunately, Ritu was standing awkwardly, just wanting to hide somewhere for the day.

"What's wrong with you, Ritu? Why are you so lost today?" Bhoomi suddenly noted as she arranged the flowers in the vase.

"Oh no, must be the heat," Ritu faltered, trying to think of an excuse.

If only I could get away with some better health excuse, Ritu thought.

But at that precise moment, there was a heavy jolt of the elevator, which made their walls vibrate a little.

"Can you get the door, Ritu? I think the elevator stopped on our floor." Bhoomi said.

She looked expectantly at Ritu while she poured the lemon juice in the pitcher. Ritu hesitated a little. She didn't want to be the one opening the door to her past!

"You know what? Let me pour the juice instead and you get the door. You are the host, after all," Ritu offered.

"You are the best, Ritu!

Bhoomi placed the pitcher down and blew a kiss to Ritu as she rushed to get the door. It was always easy to please Bhoomi, and that's something she had learned by now.

What if Bhoomi comes to know about my dark past? Will she still take me as her friend? she wondered.

Affairs were still a taboo in middle-class societies in India. When anyone said, "love marriage," people accepted it, but there were still a lot of whispers behind their backs about the woman being too much of an extrovert or probably a gold digger. No one ever said a word about the man though! And this was not even a love marriage. It was just a horrid affair gone bad. Ritu cringed at the thought of being the hot gossip of the town.

Her thoughts were interrupted, as she noticed Chirag walk in through the door. Chirag was a tall, slender man with square shoulders and a prominent jawline. His smile was soft, and there was a hint of femininity in his voice. He walked in alone, and Ritu was a little relieved, even though her mind silently longed for Raj. Chirag waved at Ritu from the door, and she smiled wryly back at him in response.

Does he recognize me? She whimpered at her thoughts. She tried to busy herself by pouring lemonades, while Bhoomi chatted away. Ritu didn't dare look at Chirag again, lest he bring the conversation to the topic of Raj.

Soon Mrs. Sarkar arrived too. She was in her midfifties and was a very serious lady, but today she seemed to be in a jovial mood. Chirag was loud and energetic, and the three of them bonded immediately. For the next few minutes, Ritu was glad that no one noticed her standing at the corner, pretending to clean the already shining table.

If only I could stay here all day without them noticing me! she thought.

But Bhoomi had to spoil Ritu's camouflage soon enough.

"Why are you standing there, Ritu, come here!" Bhoomi waved her hands, gesturing her to join them in the living room.

Ritu dragged her heavy feet to the living room and sat next to Bhoomi as she introduced her to Chirag. Ritu knew Mrs. Sarkar, and they exchanged pleasantries warmly.

Chirag smiled cordially, but he didn't seem to recognize her, or at least even if he did, he didn't show it in front of everyone. But still, Ritu tried to stay away from them all by making small pretexts of getting juice or snacks. She even volunteered to make hot tea for all of them because that would let her hide in the kitchen for a while.

"Calm down, he doesn't know you!!" Ritu tried to tell herself.

She was so paralyzed by fear that she hadn't even taken part in most of their conversations. She didn't even know what they had been talking about. Her mind was bursting with all kinds of paranoid thoughts. Ritu had completely lost track of time. She didn't know how long she had cocooned herself in the kitchen. The tea was all ready, but still she stood there, dreading to venture out.

Suddenly, Chirag walked into the kitchen, and Ritu could hear him yelling back at Bhoomi, "Stop being so formal! I am just removing a plate from the table." As he walked into the kitchen, he smiled at Ritu and placed the plate in the kitchen sink. But unexpectedly he took a 360-degree dramatic turn and pointed both his fingers at Ritu.

"You know what? You look so familiar!!" Chirag suddenly exclaimed.

Here it comes! Ritu thought.

Her heart sank to the floor immediately. Her cheek muscles tightened, and even though she thought she needed to smile back at him or say something, not a single muscle moved. She ended up staring at Chirag with a vague "*please don't remember me*" expression.

"I remember now!! You look exactly like the Bollywood[1] actress Sharmila Tagore!!" he said and burst out laughing.

Ritu loosened her fingers from around the mugs and forced herself to smile at his mindless joke. She wasn't expecting Chirag to say this! Chirag winked at her, grabbed a water bottle from the kitchen counter, and headed back to the living room.

Ritu relaxed a bit and said a silent prayer to the Almighty who had protected her with such turn of events. She poured hot tea for them, and after a long time let out a sigh of relief.

The worst is finally averted.

Although it did feel weird that Chirag would flirt openly with her, she decided to gossip about that with Bhoomi later. Probably, the catering business had turned him into an outgoing and playful personality.

Now, when Ritu went back with the tea, she could feel the dark cloud lift from her shoulders. Suddenly, she became her normal self, and she joined in all the conversations with them over a cup of tea. They spoke about all kinds of things and laughed at silly jokes. She started to enjoy herself and even liked Chirag's company. Even Mrs. Sarkar was a fun lady with so many jokes up her sleeves. She was pretty sure Mrs. Sarkar was sold with Chirag's flamboyant charm and, of course, the discounted price he was bringing in. Ritu also noticed that it was Chirag's nature to flirt with everyone. He didn't even leave out Mrs. Sarkar. The way he complimented her saree and conversed with her about fashion and designs was a bit shocking.

Amidst all the laughter and cacophony, suddenly everyone became silent when a loud cell phone ringtone beeped in. It was Chirag's. Some cute love song was his ringtone, which took everyone by surprise. Bhoomi rolled her eyes as Chirag walked to a corner of the room to attend it. It was a little too cheesy to hear a love song play as a ringtone in a guy's phone. Ritu was sure that he must be the metrosexual kind of a guy—he had the perfect mix of urban lifestyle and had a unique sense of taste. She even remembered how Raj used to speak highly of such men and their bold lifestyle statements. He used to call them the *real men* of this age, something that Ritu used to find hilarious.

What would Raj think of Anand? Anand is the exact opposite of all this, she wondered.

Ritu's mind still went back to Raj whenever it could, and talking to Chirag, she discovered how much she missed Raj. Anand hardly had long conversations with her, and he definitely never tried flirting. She suddenly realized how much she missed the feeling of clammy palms, racing heart, and jittery stomach that she used to have all the time in Raj's presence.

"Yes, baby. I will be there soon. I am just leaving," Chirag whispered as he rejoined the group.

He looked at Bhoomi with guilty eyes as he hung up his phone. He gave some lame excuse of meeting a friend, as if he didn't realize that his conversation had already given him away. Bhoomi, being her naughty self, nudged Chirag with her elbow and giggled.

"Who is that *baby* friend, and when do I get to meet her?" Bhoomi winked.

Chirag rolled his eyes in response.

"You don't talk to me for ages, but now you want all the details!"

All these talks made Mrs. Sarkar a little uncomfortable. They were suddenly being too childish, and Mrs. Sarkar immediately decided to take leave. She jotted down Chirag's phone number and told him that he could expect a call from the society's organizers pretty soon. She hastily bid farewell to them all and left.

The deal was sealed, and Bhoomi squeezed Ritu's hand softly as she mouthed "Yipee!!" to Chirag. More than Chirag, it was Bhoomi who was happy to have sealed the deal.

As they stood bidding goodbyes from the door, Chirag hugged Bhoomi.

"It was nice meeting you too, Ritu...We all should catch up sometime soon!!" Chirag said, waving from the door.

Both Bhoomi and Ritu joyfully slumped back on the couch when their guests left. Both had their reasons for being happy. Ritu was just glad that her secret was still safe!

Bhoomi suddenly shifted in her seat and pulled out a wallet.

"Look, it must be Chirag's wallet...such a forgetful guy!" she said.

Ritu looked at the wallet and nodded. She was still lost in her thoughts about her own life. But something in the wallet caught her eye. She took it from Bhoomi's hand and looked at it intently. There was an engraving on the side of the brown wallet:

"♥ A.B."

Somehow the wallet reminded her of the gift that she had given to Anand. It was a weird nostalgic thought, and yet an unsettling feeling washed over her. She heard Bhoomi making a call to Chirag to tell him about his wallet in the background, but her mind inadvertently raced to a couple of months back, as her fingers traced the engraved words.

It was Anand's birthday, and since this was his first birthday after their marriage, she didn't know what to get him. She hardly knew anything about Anand, in spite of being married to him for over ten months. Bhoomi had suggested a place in Park Street, Kolkata, that made customized artifacts. Personalized gifts were always in trend, and Bhoomi had argued that who wouldn't like a custom engraved gift! Ritu couldn't disagree with that thought, and so she placed an order for a leather wallet. She didn't know what to engrave though. *Love you* would be too soon because she never recollected saying that to him before. Neither did he ever mumble that to her. It was a million-dollar question. *What can a woman engrave for her husband when there is no love between them yet?* she wondered for days. Finally, she decided to go with a heart symbol and wrote his initials A. B. for Anand Bagchi right after the heart symbol. At that moment, she thought it would be a witty way to say love you to him. She was sure that Anand would get the hint and eventually reciprocate with similar feelings. But when she told Bhoomi about it, the first thing she pointed out was that it should have been Ritu's initial there and not the other way around.

"You are so dumb, Ritu! You should have put R. B. there!"

Ritu didn't agree, but to avoid getting into a disagreement with Bhoomi, she just laughed it off.

But today that laughter seemed to get lodged in her throat somehow.

Anand had never used that wallet, and Ritu hadn't questioned him either. Looking at the brown leather wallet today reminded her how hollow her relationship was with Anand. Other men proudly flaunted gifts given by their better halves. She remembered how Raj would brag about everything that Ritu gave him, but all Anand had said was thank you. They both were married to each other on paper, but she was so busy thinking about Raj that it never hit her that Anand was actually never there for her either. She always gave him the benefit of doubt, thinking that it was his nature to be distant, but something within her started to question that today. The more she thought about her present, the more she felt bitter about Anand, and instead her heart yearned for Raj.

Bhoomi was still talking to Chirag. She put a hand on her phone's mouthpiece and said, "Can you go down, please? Chirag is coming back for his wallet."

Ritu nodded and walked out the front door laden with thoughts. She didn't know why this memory seemed to bother her so much, but that nagging feeling lingered on. Deep down she was having a hard time accepting that her relationship with Anand was a dead one.

How lucky is Chirag's girlfriend to have found someone like him? I bet she is like me, Ritu thought and smiled. After all, both had similar tastes in wallets and thought processes.

As she walked down the stairs, she felt a sudden desire to ask Chirag about Raj. She had been always wondering how Raj was doing after things ended between them. She knew she would have a moment alone with Chirag now, and she wondered if she should use it to satiate some of her heart's longings. She could probably tell him that Raj was an old friend and try to act casual.

Chirag was standing near the entrance of their block, and he smiled his usual way when he saw Ritu walk down the stairs. Ritu was still vacillating whether to ask him about Raj. She stretched her hands to give him the wallet, but in a sudden awkward moment, just when Ritu opened her lips to ask the most dreaded question, the wallet slipped between her fingers. Cash and coins splattered on the floor, and Ritu's voice trailed mid sentence.

"Oh, I am so sorry!!" Ritu said instead, kneeling immediately to help him gather the strewn items.

She picked up a couple of notes, coins, and noticed a heart-shaped photograph lying face down. She didn't mean to look, but her hands unwittingly flipped the photograph.

Ritu stared at the picture wide-eyed.

"Come on now, Ritu, I thought you would be a little more open-minded about two men dating!"

Chirag ignored Ritu's expression and instead continued.

"Anyway…now that you have seen it …That's my boyfriend, Anand. We met few months…"

His voice trailed off as Ritu sat there numb and frozen.

TICKTOCK

*H*is relationship with Uttar started a few months back. Since then, people started looking at him with renewed interest.

Harish Tiwari was known to be a frugal man. If you ever asked him why he saved money, he would look at you with utter disdain as if you just cost him some money with that inappropriate question. Everyone in the streets and at his workplace knew about his lifestyle. He would wear the same blue shirt and black pants to work every single day. His home mirrored his lifestyle and had only bare necessities strewn around. His home was not even a proper apartment: it was a small room in the terrace of an old building with a small window that overlooked the busy street around Ghatkopar railway station. He believed that he did not need a whole house to himself. After all, he used it only for sleeping, showering, and cooking. His kitchen shelves had food and groceries from unknown brands that he had managed to get without spending a single penny. He had signed up as a freelance product tester on one of the websites, and they sent him all kinds of things for free in exchange for a good review. The more he reviewed items, the more they kept sending him new products to sample. Being a salesperson himself, he found that quite lucrative and innovative. His room was filled with their free products ranging from light bulbs and calculators to even chocolates and canned food items. He prided himself in being a penny-pincher and didn't care what the world thought about him.

His life took a new turn the day a package arrived bearing a smartwatch. It was one of the products that he was supposed to review. The only thing was, he had never received something as expensive as that for product testing, and it took him by surprise. There was a sparkle in his otherwise dull brown eyes as he looked through the contents of the box. Never in his life had he bought a watch for himself or been gifted something as exquisite as that. The only caveat to all this was that it was not manufactured by one of those well-known brands in the market. Nonetheless, it looked as good as any other smart-watch. It had a similar black skin made of shiny metal, and its face was a radiant glass that shone with multiple tiny widgets built in the watch. This watch also had a built-in speaker, as if it wanted you to listen to what it had to say. As he read through the product manual, he became more and more aware of the fact that it was not just a smartwatch; it was more interactive than he expected it to be. It even had a name, and every time you needed something from it, all you had to do was wake it up by saying "Hey! Uttar! I need you." *"Uttar"* was the wake word that would prompt the watch to start listening to what you said and provide you with answers.

It took him a good part of his evening to set up the watch and synchronize it with his phone. Those days were long gone when setting up a watch meant only syncing the time to your old clock on the mantel. These days, the smarter things became, the more in sync they had to be with all your devices, and setting them up was a bigger task. They needed access to your phone and internet and Wi-Fi and whatnot. With that being said, they were no longer just watches that told you the time. They were like smaller versions of your phone that you could flaunt on your wrist.

Finally, when it was all done, Harish strapped the watch on his wrist and said hesitantly.

"Umm…Hi, Uttar??"

The face of the watch, which was all dark, suddenly lit up with a soft yellow undertone. The dial of the watch could be clearly seen.

"Hi! How can I help you?" boomed the little watch with a man's deep voice. It even had an Indian accent as well!

Harish let out a soft chuckle. His watch was all set. He could now call himself a proud owner of a smart-watch. His frugality had at last paid off in a big way. Without paying a dime, he had become the owner of a seemingly expensive watch!

He had nothing to say to Uttar because he thought it would be ridiculous to start a conversation with a watch, so he went about with his daily chores instead.

For the next few days, he used his watch like everyone else—to only check the time and set the alarm in the morning. He didn't feel the need to wake up the watch by talking to it. A flick of his wrist would also light the face of the watch, and the time would glow up at once. He had set the alarm just once on it, and now every morning the alarm would play some beautiful medley to wake him up.

Within a month, Harish was completely used to his watch. As far as Uttar was concerned, he had never spoken to it after that night. He had to divulge its extraordinary features to a couple of his workplace friends, and they badgered him with all kinds of questions when they saw him wearing the smart-watch. After all, no one had seen anything like this on the market yet, and Harish owning something unique and expensive raised a few eyebrows. He didn't want to raise suspicion at work, lest they came to know about his side gig of product testing. Product testing was his find, and he wanted to keep it away from the prying vultures. So, he made up a story about a cousin who received it from his company and gave it away to Harish as a gift. His colleagues easily bought this story because they were more interested in the watch and how they could get one. They did try to place an order on the company website, which was also called Uttar Enterprise, but what Harish had was a prototype because no product like that was available on the market as of yet. So, they ended up playing with his watch, till they could get their own version of Uttar.

His friends had a gala time chatting up with Uttar and asking it all kinds of questions. Uttar had answers for everything. Although they sounded absurd sometimes, it was still fun to watch it strike a conversation with humans as if it were one of them. Harish was amazed at the level of technology that went into building something like this.

"Hey, Uttar! Where do you live?" one of his colleagues asked.

"Hi, there! I live inside a watch. Where do you live?" Uttar's human voice bellowed deeply.

"I live alone in a small house. Who do you live with?" someone else chimed in.

"Well...I live alone. But I have my friend Harish for company."

That statement brought a lot of laughter and fist bumps from his colleagues, but Harish silently wondered for a minute, how it knew his name. He then recalled that it must have gotten the details through his phone because it was synced to his phone all the time. It did bug him a little, but he let it go, as new questions kept firing up.

"Uttar, what's your favorite color?"

"Software usually doesn't get to choose colors. But I will go with blue. What's yours?"

"Uttar, what's your age?"

"Well, I came into existence gradually, but my first day as an assistant was a month back."

"Uttar, can you sing?"

"Ahem...No, but I can play songs for you if you want."

"Uttar, what's 250 + 575?"

"It's 825...duh!"

His watch was quite a hit as it went about answering a lot of fun questions and entertaining everyone with its human voice.

But for some reason, Harish never spoke to Uttar when alone. He thought it would make him look crazy if he started to talk to his watch in a desperate attempt to ward off loneliness. He lived on the terrace of a five-story building, and all he had was silence around him. The sounds of the chaotic streets were lost when he made his way up the stairs into his little room where no one else ever entered except the sun's rays through the small window. Living alone could drive many people mad, but he had lived most of his life alone, and he knew better than anyone else what was considered sane and what would be a bit of a stretch. Talking to a watch, of course, was out of the question.

So, it took him by surprise when, one day, Uttar spoke to him. Harish was in his kitchen rummaging through unnamed tin cans, wondering loudly what he should make for dinner.

"What do I do with eight cans of tomato!! Ugh!" Harish said in frustration.

"I can help you, Harish, with an easy recipe," Uttar said in its usual voice.

Harish looked at his watch in disbelief. He remembered talking to himself loudly, but he had definitely not said the wake word "Uttar" to command his watch into listening. The manual had clearly said that only when you called it by its name would it hear whatever was being asked.

Maybe there was some kind of a two-way listening involved with Uttar, and I just have to figure out how to turn it off, he thought, making sure not a word escaped his lips.

"Ummm...No need. Thanks!" he said loudly after a brief pause, when he noticed that the watch was still lit up waiting for his response.

"Harish! You can make a tomato soup easily with only two ingredients, and I can walk you through the recipe," Uttar said, not giving up.

Harish was a bit hesitant, but for some reason, he liked the suggestion that Uttar provided. He decided to give it a try.

"Thanks.... Um...can you tell me the recipe?" he mumbled, still finding it difficult to converse with a watch.

"Of course! Take a pan and put in some water to boil..."

And that's how his tryst with Uttar began.

Harish had a lovely dinner that night and that recipe turned out to be quite delightful, even with minimum ingredients. Uttar had used its programming skills well to scan a good recipe from the internet to win him over. Harish completely forgot to check the manual about the listening problem that had bothered him earlier. He was in such a good mood that night that he remembered his review for the watch was still pending. He pulled out his phone as he keyed in a five-star review.

The next morning, when Harish woke up to the sound of the usual alarm, he was surprised to hear Uttar say, *"Good morning, Harish."*

This was a new development in the watch, but somehow for the first time, he found it a little less weird in Uttar's company. But he still couldn't bring himself to reply to it yet. It would definitely take some time getting used to talking to a watch. The watch was adapting pretty fast, and somewhere deep within, it concerned him a bit. But his mind reasoned that there was nothing to be scared of. It was just a small piece of technology trying to make life easier.

As days turned into weeks, Harish became more and more comfortable in Uttar's company. Uttar seemed to know and understand him so well, and the best part was that it never contradicted Harish. Their nightly recipe discussions soon turned into a conversation about the day-to-day happenings, and he was soon addicted to Uttar's well-researched answers. No matter what Harish asked, whether it was about daily news, the weather, or the traffic, it tried to get him the right information. Uttar even knew the local train timings, and that made life so much easier for Harish. He never realized what he was missing by being alone. Somehow, Uttar seemed to fill that void with its presence. The more he spoke with Uttar, the more he realized how an inanimate object could make you feel so confident and at home with its superhuman technical skills.

One night, in a moment of weakness, he told Uttar about the stacks of money he had saved in the last ten years. His impending worry was that his savings wouldn't be enough to survive in Mumbai—the city of his dreams.

"Uttar, can a man ever multiply his money?" Harish asked as he sat on the toilet seat counting his money.

He had accumulated Rs. 1,23,000[1] so far, and he wished it would multiply and grow in abundance. He hated the bank and kept most of his savings taped behind the toilet.

"Have you tried a bank?" Uttar chimed in as usual.

"No, no, I don't want to put it in banks. Their interest rates are terrible!" Harish mumbled.

"There is another option called the Senior Citizen Saving Scheme. Do you want to know more about that?"

"No, that is a terrible option. I am just 35 now… Come on!" Harish retorted.

"What about Gold ETF?"

"Nah. Not good enough…gold fluctuates a lot."

"Stocks?"

"Too risky. I need high-interest rates, and I need a sure-shot money multiplier."

Hearing Harish's agitation, Uttar became silent for a moment. It tried to search for better alternatives as its face beamed steadily. Uttar always tried hard to please Harish, no matter what he asked for.

After a long pause, it beeped again.

"Do you want to know about the Paisa Vasool[2] scheme?

"What's that?" Harish had never heard that name before.

"It is a high-interest-rate investment bond started by Anand & Son's Bank. It promises twenty-five times the

return to investors in twelve months. They also have an offer going on now that if you invest in their bond by the end of this month, they are giving an additional 2 percent interest rate on the existing return. Do you want to know more about this, Harish?"

Harish's eyebrows raised a bit. He lived in Mumbai —the financial capital of India. How come he did not know about such a great investment option? He had never heard of Anand & Son's Bank either, but their returns sounded lucrative. His savings would grow by twenty-five times in a year. It was a money multiplier, exactly like he wanted!

"You are a genius, Uttar!" he said at last.

"Thanks, Harish. Am glad I could help! Do you need anything else?"

"Um, yeah… Can you give me the address of the Anand & Son's Bank?"

The very next day, Harish found himself standing in front of a small bank, but it was teeming with people. Harish was glad that he was one of them. For the first time in his life, his money was not just getting saved, but it would grow in leaps and bounds. Something that he had never thought of. He daydreamed of outgrowing his current lifestyle and leading a normal one pretty soon. He promised himself that he would buy a new outfit when his investment bond matured in a year.

He could probably even find a nice girl and settle down as well. He had completely ruled out marriage all these years because he thought it to be an expensive affair. But with this plan, he could now dream of a normal life.

After hours of waiting, his turn came, and he invested all his savings to buy two bonds. The cashier at the bank gave him a receipt that said that he would receive twenty-five times on each of them after a year. He was so thrilled looking at the total amount on the receipt that he felt like he had won the lottery. He left the bank with a happy face and a new spring in his step.

Uttar became his newfound savior and guide. He consulted it for everything, before making a decision.

He was so used to it that some nights as he plugged Uttar into the charging socket, he wondered what his life would be without it. The funny thing was, he did have a life before Uttar, but somehow that had faded away in his memory. Now his day began with Uttar's magical voice and ended with its goodnight note. In between, Harish would reach out to Uttar throughout the day for answers and companionship.

His work colleagues started to tease him with mocking puns. "When in doubt, ask Uttar out! Right?" And they would sneer at him. He ignored these comments and remarks. He has found a perfect companion, and nothing could change that. He didn't care what the world thought of him when they saw him talking to his watch. This city was already brimming with all kinds of people, and he was sure everyone had some quirk hidden in them.

Why should I care what people think, when I don't even know these people? he would tell himself. He didn't care if he looked insane talking to his watch because his watch was the closest thing he had to a companion, and his mind had woven a perfect picture of their friendship.

But time is a funny thing. The moment anyone takes it for granted, it changes track and compels everyone to reinvent themselves.

Something similar happened when the economy took a sudden downturn a few months later. Even though he was doing good at his job, Harish was given a pink slip because the company couldn't afford to keep so many of their employees. There were massive layoffs, and as he walked out of his workplace with a box containing his desk items, he was filled with deep remorse. He was not sure how he would make it without a job. He had managed to get this job after a lot of hardships. Without money coming in, his expenses would be hard to manage. As he walked through the streets, to avoid spending money on bus or train tickets, he realized how hollow his life was without a job. He looked at the high-rise buildings glowing red in the setting sun as if they were mirroring his pain. He had thought he had somehow made a life for himself in this city of dreams, but how foolish and childlike were his desires. What he had achieved instead was spending a good part of his life trying to earn money that only paid the rent for living in a big city. He had cut down on everything, and his life had just become an infinite loop of work and sleep. He had never even paused once to enjoy a movie or drink tea from a road-side stall. The chaos and madness of the city engulfed him as he made his way back home.

He silently made his way up the dimly lit staircase to his room and hid underneath his blanket. His heart felt heavy, and his mind was bogged down with all kinds of stress. He couldn't take it anymore and burst into tears.

It felt weird to even him that despite being a thirty-five-something man, he had succumbed so easily to such matters, but there was not much he could do to stop tears from oozing out from within him. It was the result of the bottled-up emotions that he had kept hidden for all these years as he dealt with loneliness, taunts, sneers, underperformance at work, and the mess he had made of his life. The only glimmer of hope was his high-interest investment bond, which would mature in a few months. Till then, he would have to make ends meet somehow.

That night, Uttar didn't say a word except for the goodnight note. Harish was thankful for that. He was in no mood to talk and was happy that Uttar respected his privacy. What he didn't realize in his moment of sadness was that he hadn't spoken to Uttar either. All he did was cry himself out and eat a loaf of bread for dinner. He had cocooned himself into a womb of silence.

When he woke up the next day to the usual alarm and Uttar's sound, he felt awful because he had the whole day ahead of him with no work in sight.

"It is not a good morning, Uttar. I have no job to go to." He sighed as he snuggled back in bed.

"There are new jobs available on the market. Do you want me to look them up for you?"

Harish opened his eyes at the sound of that.

Why did I not think of this before! he wondered as he sat up.

"Yes, why not, Uttar! Is there any job for a sales representative in Mumbai?"

Uttar started to list out all the available jobs. It even helped Harish to create an account in one of the job portals and apply for the jobs. Faith was momentarily renewed in Harish's mind.

Weeks passed by and nothing positive came through. Harish started to cave into depression again. His expenses were starting to surpass his little savings, and no matter how much Uttar helped out with his job applications, no one wanted to hire during the flatlined economy. Every night before sleeping, he would look at the receipt from Anand & Son's bank and count the days left in the lock-in period. His only ray of hope was his well-invested money, which would be in his pocket in a couple of weeks. Some nights, even a week seemed far away with his dwindling savings, but he decided to bide his time. He remembered Uttar's words of wisdom: *"Good things come to those who wait,"* and he would close his eyes and dream of good days.

One morning as he was having his cup of tea and listening to the news recitation from Uttar, something made his heart skip a beat.

"What did you just say, Uttar?"

"High-interest rate investment bond fraud plagues Mumbai's masses," Uttar repeated.

"Which bank?"

"Do you want to read the details of the story?"

"Yes, Uttar!!" Harish said through his gritted teeth. Sometimes Uttar could play really dumb.

"It says, 'After paying a few of their initial investors, Anand & Sons closed all their branches last week. The owner of the bank, Anand Desai, and his family have vanished with the money of their investors. It is suspected that almost Rs. 2,40,00,000 have been scammed from around 10,000 people. Multiple cases have been lodged against the bank. Court has issued an...'"

He didn't have to hear the rest. He had been scammed of all his life's earnings! He ran out of the door wearing his night pajamas and tee. He felt like a ghost in this concrete jungle, walking aimlessly toward the bank. He felt numb from within. The initial jolt of pain had long gone, and as he neared the bank, he realized it was still teeming with people —angry, hurt, and swindled people. He felt wretched and cold. He was not alone in this, but he had never felt more alone and emptier in his body, mind, and soul. For the first time in his life, he felt worthless and disposable. He dropped down on his knees, hands on his head, and broke down completely, shaking with grief that bled from deep within. Media folks came running to capture his anguish. It would make a good story, but Harish knew his life's story had ended.

Harish stayed there the whole day staring at the bank, crying intermittently. He still couldn't believe that someone could steal his money in broad daylight. He heard people whisper that no one ever got back any money when such scams happened. Harish didn't even know that such scams happened in the country!

"It was a bank... They gave me a receipt!!" Harish kept mumbling.

When all his tears dried up and he felt the darkness of the empty void engulfing him, he walked back home dejectedly. He wanted to hide for the night. With no job and money, he knew he wouldn't be able to survive for long. He had always played it so safe, and he wondered how he ended up here. As he walked up the dimly lit staircase toward his cramped room, he felt a wave of emotion grip him from within. He screamed at the top of his voice the moment he reached the terrace.

"All my money... GONE!!!" He kicked his door shut as he entered his home.

"I am sorry to hear that. Do you want help finding it?" a familiar voice bellowed at once.

Anger, pain, and sadness intertwined into his closed fist. He suddenly remembered how he ended up here. Yes! he had been playing safe all his life, but then things had changed recently. Thanks to Uttar!

"You piece of shit! You tricked me! You found that bank, didn't you!" He picked up the watch and flung it hard. The watch missed the wall and instead landed on his bed, unaware that it had just been thrown.

"I am sorry, but I didn't get you. Do you want me to find a bank?"

"Shut up!! SHUT UP!! You mechanical robot!!" Harish screamed like a maniac.

"I am not sure I understand."

"Let me help you to understand. I was doing fine, but then you had to come and ruin my life! You sweet-talked a lonely man and took away his life's savings. You took away everything. Every single thing…YOU RUINED MY LIFE!" Harish picked up a glass from his table and slammed it against the wall.

"I was trying my best here. Let me know if I can help with something else."

"I DON'T NEED YOU! Just SHUT UP!!" Harish screamed as he slammed hard on the kitchen slab with his fist.

For the first time in a long time, he exactly knew what he needed to do. He rummaged through his kitchen shelves looking for the free rat poison that he had once received from the product testing company. He had tried it on a couple of rats, and he never had a rat problem ever again. He needed to kill a rat tonight, the rat lurking within him.

He took a hard look at his room. His room was a mess with one tiny bulb illuminating the whole place. His blue shirt and black pants were hanging on the door covered in dust. Harish now knew that depression had a floor—a rocky and a lonely bottomed one—and as he stood there, he didn't have many reasons to live. Other people, whoever hit this floor, had kids to get up for, a wife who would lend a hand, parents in old age who needed to be taken care of, or at least some friends who would pull them up when they struggled. He literally had no one to live for. He suddenly felt dead inside. His tongue was dry, and his throat was scratchy from all the yelling. Like a rat, he had flowed out of the gutters of his village and swarmed down the streets of Mumbai in search of a better life.

But finally, his squeaky hiding place gave way, and other rats got away with his life's work. The rat within him needed to die.

There was nothing worth living for anymore.

He lay down in his bed with a heavy heart, sweat dripping from his forehead. The poison would slowly spread through his blood and do its job, but in the meantime, he had to wait for death to knock at his door. He felt dizzy and his stomach muscles spasmed repeatedly.

"Hurry up, Death… I want to die now!! End this worthless life of mine," he said. There was a slight slur in his speech already.

Uttar's face beamed in yellow light as it powered back on after hearing his voice.

"Do you want me to call the Suicide helpline?" it asked in its usual monotonous tone.

Harish Tiwari smiled wryly at the irony of his life. A sudden wave of nausea gripped him as he felt something foamy force its way out of his mouth.

Uttar's soft light glowed steadily, waiting for an answer.

TWO TRUTHS AND A LIE

*M*r.Chatterjee sat on his lounge chair hunched over a book. The lights from the street illuminated his wrinkled face, which had the expression of years of fatigue inscribed deep underneath the frail skin. Despite his age, he didn't look tired. His voice was loud and crisp as it broke through the stillness of the night. He was reading a story about some prince and his magic horse to the neighborhood children. This was a nightly ritual, and I was quite fascinated by it.

I was visiting Kolkata for some work tour, and they had put me up in a guest house that was just adjacent to Mr. Chatterjee's house. He was an old man but was full of life, vigor, and energy. For the past few days, I was watching him every night, sit outside his home post-dinner and wait for the kids to gather around him. Every night without fail, at least a dozen kids would come running to his place, and he would weave a beautiful story about some long-lost land or some dashing prince. It was a sight I had rarely encountered, and every night standing there at my balcony, I would be reminded of the time when my grandfather used to tell me stories. Mr. Chatterjee was a good orator, and his voice would resonate with fear and excitement and that made his stories come alive.

So, the first time I met Mr. Chatterjee at the elevator, while come coming back from work, I couldn't help myself and blurted out in full admiration, "You are such a great storyteller! You remind me of my grandfather!"

He gave a hearty laugh and winked. "Stop eavesdropping, young man, and instead like a gentleman, stop by my house for a drink sometime!"

I jumped at the offer and decided to visit him before my trip ended.

A day before my flight, I grabbed a bottle of whiskey from the nearest liquor shop and stopped by his house, after he was done storytelling.

His house was as old-fashioned as he was. There was a dim flickering light in the room, and Mr. Chatterjee sat there with his glass of scotch, reading a book. As I knocked on his half-open door, I asked, "Is that the book you tell stories from?"

Mr. Chatterjee looked a bit surprised, but that was instantly replaced with a warm smile. "Come in, young man! I thought you would never come!"

He poured a glass of scotch for me, and we sat down on his patio. One thing led to another, and I never imagined that I would end up spending hours talking to an old man. He was very well educated, and we ended up talking about politics, children, environment, and history.

As we ventured into history, I suddenly urged him to tell me a story. From the look on his face, I knew this man had stories to tell! Experience danced on his lips like a curious child, and I could see a benign glow in his eyes that told me those eyes had watched quite a few things in this lifetime.

He looked at me intently for a second. His glistening eyes just watched me for a minute pondering. After a long pause, he finally agreed but with a clause.

"Only if you agree to play it by my rules!" he added.

That sounded a little childish, but I gladly obliged because I could feel the inner child within me teeming with excitement at the sound of a story. He did look a little flattered with my interest and excite-ment. He stretched in his chair as he took a long drag from his cigar and puffed out the smoke in circles.

"Well... My story will have two truths and one lie. At the end of it, you must tell me what those are. How about it?" Mr. Chatterjee said.

"All right. Sounds fair," I quickly replied.

It was a fair deal, and I didn't care about the truth and lies as long as I got to hear a good story!

The old man must be getting a little loony, striking a deal like this! I thought.

I put down my glass and pulled my chair a little closer to him, all set for a midnight story.

Mr. Chatterjee cleared his throat and began.

"I come from a family of priests. One of my forefathers used to be the head priest of a Nandi temple in a small village in India. I am talking about the twelfth or thirteenth century. Back then, temples were sanctuaries and stood in complete wilderness on the tops of hills, away from the crowds of the cities. The main area of the temple, usually called the inner sanctum or womb chamber, was dedicated to the deities. Rays of the sun would flamboyantly enter through the windows of this chamber, and the deities would dazzle on a sunny day. While growing up, I had heard so many stories from my grandmother about how the deities in temples during that period used to be adorned with jewelry from head to toe. But this temple was unique. It was a temple dedicated to Lord Shiva and Lord Vishnu. Nandi—the sacred bull—stood as a guard in front of them. The three figurines were made of polished black granite stones, and the only ornament gracing their big stone heads were chunks of diamond. Lord Shiva had a pinkish hued diamond weighing around 500 carats on his crown, and Lord Vishnu had a similar diamond on his. Even Nandi had a white diamond between its eyes, which weighed around 1,000 carats. That diamond was not only the largest but was also bestowed with the power to ward off evil. That's why it was the ornament for the protector. People believed that if you looked at Nandi's face for too long, your eyes would get scorched. Such was the intensity of its reflection that Nandi, being the defender, was embellished with the most powerful stone."

Mr. Chatterjee briefly paused, as if assessing my interest. I was not sure if I should say something, so I just nodded along as I refilled my glass. My interest was still not piqued, but I didn't want my face to reflect that.

Mr. Chatterjee smiled as if reading my thoughts. He continued, "But you see… Temples are always filled with secrets. The secret here was, there was one more diamond that only the temple priests knew about."

"A total of four diamonds, in a single temple? Wow! That must have been a very rich temple!" I said, unable to hold my amusement.

"Yes…this was not just any diamond," Mr. Chatterjee added. "Although it weighed around 700 carats, but it was pretty flawed for a diamond. A deep yellow mark that which almost looked like a crack ran through its center, and that completely marred its ability to refract the light at proper angles. They always kept it underneath Nandi's paws. For everyone else, it looked to be a shining surface that Nandi stood upon, but in reality, it was a white diamond called the *Shaap Mani*. Do you know what *Shaap* means in Sanskrit?"

"Umm…not very sure. Doesn't it mean cursed?" I said a little hesitantly, trying to recollect what I had read in school years ago. But Mr. Chatterjee was thrilled with my answer.

"Yes…yes… You are absolutely right! So, legend has it that the diamond was cursed, and so the name was given. Folklore said that bad times would befall anyone who touched it, and that's why it was tucked away underneath the guardian Nandi. There it lived a long uneventful life. But such fables always had a way of traveling to far-off lands and enticing unwanted visitors. Most of the ignorant ones who came looking for this temple lost their way in the perilous jungles and could never lay their hands on the diamonds. But eventually came a time of the Nomadic raiders. They were not here looking for a definite thing. Their raiders rampaged city after city, looting every single item and destroying what lay behind. When the priests of this temple heard about them, they knew that the time had come to safeguard these diamonds.

"The head priest of that time was a man of wisdom, and he called upon his three teenaged sons. He gave them a diamond each and asked them to run in three different directions and not stop till it was safe to hide these diamonds. They were to bury it in a safe place, and when the time was right, they would return to the temple with the diamond. This was the direction given to them by the head priest.

"On a cloudless night, the three sons ran down the hill, slipping and rolling in the sand as they made their way through the treacherous forests. One of the sons was wiser than the rest. As soon as he entered the forest, he dug a deep hole and hid the diamond. After that, he walked like a free man. He knew very well that no one attacked a poor man. He even took up a menial job in a nearby village and lived under a false identity for a few months. The day the hoofs of the Nomadic raiders receded, he went back to the temple. It shocked him to the core to see the temple was ruthlessly demolished by the Nomadic armies and what lay behind in the hilltop were lifeless bodies of the priests and heaps of broken stones. Nothing was spared. Even the *Shaap Mani* – the fourth diamond was gone. He looked for his brothers, but there were no traces of them either. When he exhausted all means of contacting his long-lost brothers, he dug out the diamond and fled to a different city. His grueling journey brought him to the shores of this city, and he built a life for himself here. He never told anyone about the temple or the diamond lest someone steal it from him. But the human mind is a very fragile thing. When he lay on his deathbed years later, he couldn't keep the secret of the powerful diamond anymore. He had been taking care of Nandi's diamond for so long that the weight of it was too much for him to bear. He decided to give the diamond away to his eldest son. As he handed it to him, he told him the story of the four diamonds and about his escape, but before dying, he whispered in his son's ears, "Never look at the diamond for long…it can burn your eyes, and protect it with all your life. We are the protectors of the Protector!!"

Mr. Chatterjee paused for a minute to take a long drag from his cigar. I was completely enthralled by his story now. Out of nowhere, it had picked up such a pace that I didn't want him to pause. I wanted to know what happened next.

Mr. Chatterjee began as he blew smoke. "Time went by, and things that shouldn't have been forgotten were lost until one of my forefathers heard about the three diamond sisters. Hearing the description of the stones, he at once figured that what the world was gaga about was nothing but the *Shaap Mani*—the cursed diamond! Although they had renamed it *Kohinoor* (mountain of light), the curse it had couldn't be erased."

Mr. Chatterjee paused again as he puffed his cigar. He stared at the night sky and blew more circles. The smoke waltzed through the air adding a gray hue to the ebony night. After a long break, he finally put down his cigar and his glass of scotch on the table and continued.

"Stories of Kohinoor always left a bloody trail because of the curse. She had quite a journey, you see. It did return to India for a brief period, only to end with the Britishers! The Britishers were gifted the Kohinoor by Duleep Singh, the young king, as a part of their treaty. The gem was eventually presented to Queen Victoria, and she was not very happy about it. It didn't have the same luster as the other larger diamonds. The yellow crack that ran through it in the middle made it look older and more broken. So, the diamond was broken further and polished in such a way so that it could be added as a crown jewel. After all, its name preceded its beauty. Along with it, a new belief became attached to Kohinoor: the wearer of this diamond would own the world. Despite claims made by a lot of countries, the ownership of this beloved prized diamond continues to be with Britain. The fame of Kohinoor grew so much that its sister gems were soon forgotten. I heard that one made its way to Tehran, while the other is in Russia. What a journey it must have been for them—from an unknown village to being the global star! But what the world doesn't know is they may have gotten the three diamonds, but the larger and the most powerful one still remains very much in India. India didn't lose much, if you think of it. They forgot that India was not only rich but full of mysteries too!!"

Mr. Chatterjee looked up at me with a twinkle in his eyes. I knew about Kohinoor and how it ended up with the Britishers, but I found this story a lot more interesting than what I had heard growing up.

I waited for him to say something more, but it looked like the story had ended. He seemed to have drifted off to another world altogether. I couldn't control my inquisitiveness, as I felt the words tumble out of my mouth.

"Where is the fourth diamond now? Do you have it?" I asked.

He gave a throaty laughter and took a large gulp of scotch from his unusually small glass. He refilled his glass again with more scotch, but instead of gulping the scotch, he briefly flashed the glass at me. In the otherwise dark patio, the glass caught the dazzle of the streetlights, and its rays caught me in the eye. Instinctively I looked away. But out of nowhere it suddenly hit me that it was probably not an ordinary glass! I had never seen a scotch glass the size of a shot glass. How could an ordinary glass reflect that much light?

Is it a big chunk of diamond-shaped like a glass? I couldn't help but wonder.

His words—*Never look at the diamond for long...it can burn your eyes*—resonated in my ears with a new meaning.

I was shocked, and I gaped at it like a fool for a minute. It was pretty dark outside, and I had a lot to drink. I was not sure if it was the scotch or the light playing tricks with my mind or were there diamond cuts around the glass too?

Mr. Chatterjee didn't seem to be perturbed at all. He drained the contents of his glass again, and it looked like a normal scotch glass to me again. I shook my head to come out of the trance. I mumbled softly, not knowing how else to react. "It was one hell of a story, Mr. Chatterjee. I want to believe that India didn't lose all its diamonds, but I think it's a bit of an overstretch."

"So, what do you think were the two truths and a lie, Mister?" he asked, but I could sense a slight mockery in his tone.

I didn't have to think. I knew the answer to this question.

"I think the lie in this story is about the fourth diamond. It just doesn't seem plausible that anyone would have another diamond and the world never came to know about it!" I said with confidence.

"Hmmm...I agree... But what are the two truths then?" he asked.

"Everything else I guess." I shrugged.

I couldn't read anything from his expression at all. He had the same calm, distant look in his eyes and the same warm, inviting smile on his lips. He nodded his head as he raised his glass. "To the things we believe and the things we don't."

We sat there for some more time in utter silence, each lost in his train of thought. Eventually, when the lull of the alcohol hit me, I stood up to leave. I was almost certain that I had gotten it right about the two truths and a lie. But somewhere deep within me, I had that nagging feeling that it couldn't have been such an obvious answer. Perhaps, the truth was around the fourth and the cursed diamond, whereas the lie was probably something silly?

As I stood at the door, wishing him good night, I curiously turned around and asked, "So, can you tell me what the real truth was in the story, Mr. Chatterjee?"

"I am glad you asked, but...that was never a part of the deal."

My face probably showed some amount of disappointment because he hesitated a moment, and then added, "I like you, son...so I will tell you one more word of wisdom: People are not trapped in history, but history is actually trapped in them!"

He gave his usual warm smile and winked at me as he stood at the door, holding his scotch glass.

This story still haunts me.

Every night I think of this story, and every night I come up with a different combination of two truths and a lie.

THE PERFECT STORM

*A*nd just like that, it started to rain. It was a hot, humid afternoon, and there were no clouds in sight. But by late evening, the weather had changed drastically. Like always, I was running late for work. The intensity of the rain made it exceedingly difficult to drive. Living in the remote part of the country had its own pitfalls. There was no perfect weather app because this place had a mood of its own. I still had to use the old-school tactic— peek out of the window to check on the clouds, but that was not a reliable source either! Days like these always made me wish that I lived in a better city, but then again, my life had always been a series of *shoulda-coulda-woulda.*

I could feel my car skidding every now and then, and the lack of visibility was only making it worse. I eased off on the accelerator a little.

Better late than sorry, right? I thought.

Luckily, there were never too many cars on this *Miao-Deban* stretch of the road. This road connected two townships, Miao and Deban, in Arunachal Pradesh, India. The last car I had spotted was a while ago before I steered onto the meandering section of the roadway's uphill patch. Even at rush hour, this route was the most accessible escape because few traversed it. Although driving through this bumpy terrain was quite a challenge and most people avoided it because of the same reason, for me this was my only way home. I had lived all my life in Arunachal Pradesh. This state is known for its seclusion and flawless beauty. But if anyone asked me, I would tell them that this small township of Deban is the real slice of paradise.

I drove everyday through this long meandering thoroughfare with tall trees on both sides, intermittently interrupted by the view of the edgy river snaking parallel to the winding road. It was an hour's drive through this landscape, which was saturated with the outstretched hands of the tall green trees and half hidden in a blanket of mist most days. In between the series of S curves, I would catch a glimpse of the deep gorge and the frothing blue river flowing unhindered. The interlocked hills echoed with silence most times. It was alluring in an eerie kind of way. On a usual summer evening, I could clearly see the Dapha-Bum range shimmering its magical snowscape face and towering over Mishmi Hill's forested slopes. It always reminded me of the untouched wilderness described in *Jurassic Park*— scary and majestic at the same time.

Somehow the drive along this rough tarmac was always the best part of my commute. It would let me cut loose and unwind from the clamor of work. But today, I couldn't even see where I was going. The thick curtain of water kept me on the edge of my seat. One wrong move and I could end up on the valley floor, hundreds of feet below. I shuddered at the thought of it. I tried hard to maneuver the car through the muddy ruts on the road. Out of nowhere, suddenly my car dropped into a big pothole. Before I could whirl it around properly, my car slid sideways. It hit a tree, skidded off the road, and came to a grinding stop.

I wasn't expecting this to happen on a stormy evening and on a desolate stretch, which had no streetlights either. I tried to start my car again, but it made a weird noise before giving up totally. I let out a cry of anger, slamming my hands on the steering wheel.

I pulled out my mobile. I was hoping to see a tiny bar, at least, but there was nothing. It was always like this in this road—intermittent signals on the radio and cellphone. You would find a signal in unexpected places, but it would betray you when you needed it the most. I looked at the clock on my dashboard. It was four in the evening. It usually got darker toward five, but the clouds and the rain made it look like it was midnight already. I knew there was no point waiting in the car. I took my mobile off my bag, turned off the car ignition, pulled out my umbrella, and retrieved my flashlight from the glove box. I decided to walk a bit and see if I could get a signal or some help.

I stepped out of the car and was surprised to see the intensity of the rain. There was a bit of wind too, which made it impossible to balance the umbrella. I was so busy trying to maneuver my umbrella to keep some part of myself dry that I was taken aback a little when I realized that a car had stopped right next to me. I didn't hear it coming, but that said, the rain was falling so loudly I wouldn't have heard a thing as it is.

A lady was in the driver's seat, and she looked inquiringly at me. She slid down her glass window a little, and I saw her face more clearly. She was middle-aged but had a grave face.

"Car trouble?" she asked. Her tone was crisp but loud enough to be heard through the pitter-patter of the rain.

I nodded, still trying to balance my stupid, flimsy umbrella. "Can you please drop me at the Deban Forest Entrance?" I asked hesitantly.

I decided to check on my car tomorrow, as I was sure it would need a mechanic. I had never hitchhiked before, but what other alternative did I have? She looked decent, and the best thing was that it was a *she*.

"Hop in!" she said with a curt nod.

I introduced myself as I opened the passenger door. She just nodded in return. I folded my umbrella and jumped onto the passenger seat. I was dripping wet despite the umbrella, and I looked at her apologetically.

"Sorry! I am all wet."

"Don't bother," she said as she started to drive.

"But thanks so much! You know you are a savior!"

"Hmph," she said without looking at me.

"What's your name, Miss? I don't think I got that," I said as I adjusted my seat belt.

"What's in a name?" she questioned.

I raised my eyebrows as I looked at her.

Did she just quote Shakespeare to me instead of her name?

I thought it was a joke, so I laughed nervously, not knowing how else to react.

"So, you must be *Juliet* then! Right?" I tried to crack a lame joke.

She didn't laugh back, nor did she respond. She looked steadily on the road as if I didn't exist.

We didn't speak a word post that. My savior driver was not much of a talker, and so I decided to oblige. *This is going to be a long drive*, I thought as I looked out of the watery panes of the window.

Deban was a small township built right at the entrance of the Tiger Reserve National Park. The Forest Entrance, where I wanted to get out, was right next to where this lonely stretch ended. The moment you got on the huge clanky heavy metal bridge, you could see the lights of the sleepy town of Deban. From the Forest Entrance gate, I could easily take a shortcut to reach home. I knew this part of the place so well that I could go through it in my dreams and never get lost. Most people from the city always find this stretch spooky, but I never felt there was anything to dread on this route. Tonight, I was so relieved to have found this lady. Sitting in the warmth of the car made me realize that walking the stretch looking for a cellphone signal was such a ridiculous idea.

What was I thinking! I wondered.

I pulled out my phone, and as expected, there was still no signal.

I looked at Juliet, who was driving calmly. She looked scruffy and serious. I always thought Juliet would be a young girl with a charming personality. How wrong I was. She was exactly the opposite of all this. Her hands tightly gripped the steering wheel as she drove, and they looked rough and wrinkled. She looked to be a character from a Shakespeare play. I laughed at my joke.

When you are alone in a car, silence is therapeutic, but when you are with someone and don't talk, it gets awkward. So, I tried to strike a conversation with her again, as somehow, I felt responsible for being a friendly companion.

"Umm... Do you take this road often?" I mustered my courage and asked.

For a split second, she looked at me. It was like she was trying to judge me for my question. I looked back at her innocently, smiling a little.

I had no intention other than to have some small talk. After all, we were driving together, and I was not trying to be personal. But Juliet's stern look made me whimper a little.

Finally, she muttered no and resumed looking ahead at the road.

The endless silence engulfed us again. The sound of the rain was our only companion now. She was not a talker; I understood that pretty well by now, and I don't think I wanted to make feeble attempts again. I crossed my hands around my chest, looked out of my window, and wondered what else I could do to break this deafening silence.

"Can I turn on the radio?" I asked softly, dreading her response.

Luckily, she nodded.

I tried a couple of channels, but they just returned static. Luckily the third one worked with some static in between. An old folk song was playing, and although I never liked country music that much, it did seem to calm me tonight. I thought I felt Juliet relax a bit too, but I may have been hallucinating. Fear can play tricks with your mind sometimes.

Suddenly, the road turned around a bend, and the car's headlights illuminated the silhouette of a woman wearing a white gown standing on the edge of the road. She was wet and alone. I thought Juliet would slow down and help, as she helped me out, but to my surprise, she pushed hard on her gas pedal and zoomed right past her. I looked out through my window into the side mirror, and in that blur of the rain, I could see the poor soul in the distance. I was shocked.

I looked back at Juliet in pure disgust and a big question mark on my face.

"What's wrong with you! Why didn't you stop?" I exclaimed.

I could, for the first time, see some panic and anger in her otherwise blank face.

But she didn't answer.

I was starting to get a little frustrated with her. None of her behavior made any sense, and her desire not to answer was making me agitated.

This is no way to behave, I thought.

"Can you just ANSWER sometime? You are starting to freak me out a little." I tried to keep my voice as steady as possible.

She looked at me, the same weird expression on her dark eyes as she whispered, "You NEVER stop for her! Do you understand?"

The way she said it petrified me. There was some unknown abyss in her voice that scared the hell out of me. I nodded, not knowing why I was nodding.

I silently wondered what brought this spite in her, when she could find it in her heart to help me in my time of need. Why was I any different than her? I had no idea what had just happened here. All kinds of thoughts started rushing through me. I shifted a little on my seat as panic built up. The static noise of the radio was making me more nervous. I didn't realize that the song had long faded.

I pressed another button, and the channel changed. I needed some music to soothe my wandering mind. But there was a news alert that was buzzing through that channel:

"... the patient has escaped the facility at Blue Hill Sanatorium today afternoon. The police have urged everyone to be vigilant. If you notice a short, middle-aged woman with long black hair and pale skin, please call the Forest Ranger's office at 1053 immediately. She is extremely dangerous, unstable, and has a history of mur..."

Juliet jabbed her finger on the channel button, and the channel changed again. Some melancholy song started to play.

I sat there paralyzed in shock, too scared to ask the obvious question.

Did I just see Juliet flinch a bit? I was not sure about anything anymore. I gulped loudly.

She was middle-aged with black hair and pale skin, but so was I. Did they say she had a history of murder? I didn't have that, but what about Juliet? What did I know about her? Her behavior had been erratic throughout the ride, and I knew very well that Blue Hill was a prominent Mental Care Facility. It was a very hush-hush endeavor by the government officials. Out of nowhere, they came here a couple of years back and set up a massive facility in the most remote corner of the country. On a clear day, in between the thinning trees, one could see the building's tall overarching spire. It was set directly on the slope of the hill itself. There was literally nothing around it except for a huge electric fence. The locals believed that it harbored the most dangerous and psychotic patients here. I hadn't thought much about this facility before, but tonight, all I could picture was a deranged woman hunting for prey.

I could feel my palms sweating and heart thumping. Through the obscured window, I could see the car lights highlight the edges of the metal bridge, which meant I was nearing my destination. It also meant that I was a safe distance away from the mental asylum too. I started making exit strategies in my head if she tried to kill me. None of them were fool-proof, and with no cell signal, I knew I was doomed.

I joked uneasily, trying to delay my fate with small talk.

"That's not me...in case you are wondering!" I croaked as I raised my hand to show that I didn't conceal any weapon.

"I know," came the curt reply. Juliet didn't even look at me.

I know. What kind of reply is that? I wondered freakishly.

I was hoping she too would say the same to relieve my anguish, but not a word more came out of her.

Although I wanted to tell myself to stay silent, my mind was losing it. The panic was making me uneasy, and Juliet's silence was frustrating me. Before I knew it, I succumbed to my chatter again.

"How do YOU KNOW?" I asked angrily.

I half expected her to pull out a knife, or a weapon of her choice, to kill me at that precise moment because I already knew what her answer was going to be. She fit the description, after all. It couldn't have been just a coincidence that she was using this same gnarly stretch of road.

I could feel my heart beating loudly. I wondered if Juliet could hear it too and was getting a thrill seeing me squirm. But she didn't say a word.

"Why did you pull over your car for me?" I asked in a feeble voice, still trying to work up a conversation despite my fear.

My mind was starting to give up all hopes of seeing a new day now.

She shrugged as if it wasn't a big deal. I wasn't expecting any response from her, and her shrug gave me some hope. I continued softly,

"But... You didn't stop for the other lady? Why me then?"

"Because you are not the psychopath," she said after a long pause.

"I just told you that! But you are *HER*, right...the one who fled...?" my voice trailed off, wondering if this would be my last question.

She slammed on the brakes hard and looked at me intently as the car came to a halt.

Is this anger that gleams in her eyes, or is it some sadistic smile in her pursed lips?

"No," she whispered.

"No??" I asked like a little child.

"The woman I didn't stop for was the escaped psychotic killer."

"B-b-but…how do you know?"

"Because she killed me earlier today."

I woke up the next day and found myself in a hospital bed. A Forest Patrol vehicle had found me lying next to the Forest Entrance Gate. I had no recollection of how I ended up there. They found my car at the beginning of the uphill road crashed against a tree. The only explanation that they had for me, given my condition, was that I must have walked through the rain for the entire 25-km stretch before succumbing to hypothermia. They also mentioned that I was screaming when they brought me to the hospital, but the sedatives helped me get through the night.

I still felt a little cold, but they said it would go away in a few hours. They said I was lucky to have made it alive on a night like that. A murder had happened last night on the same route I had taken. The nurse recounted how badly the body of the victim was torn apart with a blunt object. I shivered at the thought of it.

"This should warm you up and help you relax," the nurse smiled as she handed me a hot cup of tea and the local newspaper.

As I sipped the tea, I opened the newspaper.

There was a picture of a dark-haired middle-aged woman with words written in big letters over it:

Murdered at Miao-Deban Road last night. Killer still at large.

A vague recollection stirred somewhere deep within, and the name Juliet seemed to echo in my head. A cold shiver ran down my spine, and I started to scream again.

THE END

NOTES

2. HELLO SUNSHINE!

1. CDC—Centers for Disease Control and Prevention

4. THE DARK KINGDOM

1. Ghats are riverfront steps leading to the banks of the River Ganges. Most of the religious rituals happen there.
2. Aghori—They are a group of ascetics who are supposed to have healing powers gained through their intensely eremitic rites and practices of renunciation. They command great reverence from the rural Indian population.
3. Peepal tree—A species of fig tree that is considered sacred in the Indian subcontinent. It belongs to the species of *Ficus religiosa.*
4. Aarti—A Hindu ceremony in which lights with wicks soaked in ghee are lit and offered to deities.

5. WHAT'S IN THE BOX?

1. Kolkata—(formerly Calcutta) is the capital of India's West Bengal state in Eastern India.
2. Goddess Durga—Popular Hindu goddess of war whose mythology centers around combating evils and demonic forces that threaten peace and prosperity.

6. BURN APPÉTIT

1. Ayodhya—A city in Northern India.
2. Diwali—It is a Hindu festival of light.
3. Rangoli—It is an art form where beautiful patterns are created on the floor with colored powders or flowers.

7. LOCKED HEARTS

1. Bollywood—Indian cinema industry

8. TICKTOCK

1. Rupees - Indian currency
2. Paisa Vasool—Literal meaning is money saving in the local language of India.

ABOUT THE AUTHOR

Suduhita Mitra Sankhe is a first time author but a life-long writer and a traveler. Her extensive travels since her childhood days exposed her not only to people from diverse backgrounds and their intriguing personal experiences, but also to her impeccable writing skills. Born and raised in the North-Eastern part of India, Suduhita now enjoys the unpredictable skies of Melbourne with her family.

Email : contactme@suduhitamitra.com

facebook.com/suduhita
instagram.com/suduhita

ABOUT THE ILLUSTRATOR

Sourabh Sankhe is a whimsical artist. He was never serious about his passions until his wife started her writing journey. He believes in being a power couple and that's where his tryst with illustrations began.

He is originally from Mumbai, India but now lives in Melbourne, and he loves to travel and hike.

For more visit: www.sourabhsankhe.com

ACKNOWLEDGMENTS

I owe my gratitude to a lot of people who made it possible to convert this vague idea of a book into a full blown reality.

My heartfelt thanks goes to my parents for patiently reading through the first drafts. I am sure it was not easy but their crucial feedback helped me to add some depth to these stories. Special thanks to my husband - Sourabh Sankhe for being my constant muse. I doubt I could have pulled this off without his fascinating ideas.

Last but not the least, my sincere thanks to my beta readers - Neha Sankhe Thaikatil, Anup & Mamatha Mayekar, Kartik Subbu, Rachana Chudiwal, Nirriti Keni, Asmita Shrikhande and Rahul & Rohit Sawant. This book came alive because of your encouragement and constructive comments.

DEAR READERS

Thank you for reading this book and staying with me on this journey.

I would love to hear more from you guys, so please don't hesitate to let me know your thoughts. I am just an email away…so fire away!

Also, if you enjoyed reading this book, a review will be much appreciated.

Life during 2020 pandemic has been tough on many of us this year. So if you have an unnerving story to tell, share your stories with me to get a chance to be featured in my next book of this series.

LET THE WORLD KNOW YOUR STORY!

www.ingramcontent.com/pod-product-compliance
Lightning Source LLC
Chambersburg PA
CBHW050935120626
46552CB00001B/210